Printed on Demand using CreateSpace

Cover design by Bella Clark
Beta reading by Kit Conklin, Michael Ruiz, Christian Quebral, Sunny Adams, and Ky Grabowski
Distributed by CreateSpace

ISBN: 978-1514105160 (PRINT)
ISBN: 978-1508038061 (EBOOK)

And Then There's You

by

Nessa Cannon

ACKNOWLEDGEMENTS

Thanks to Kit, Daniel, Christian, Michael, Kevin, Bella, and just about everyone I talked to over the last six months. I'm also sorry to Kit, Daniel, Christian, Michael Kevin, and just about everyone I talked to over the last six months.

I couldn't have done it without you.

Chapter One

Her dad always called it her bad wing. "The best birds have one wing bigger than the other. Like, uh..." Peter scratched his head absentmindedly. "Remember Nemo? He wasn't a bird, though, I know that. He had some whole sea adventure and didn't let anything stop him. No damn seagulls, no damn starfish, no damn shoulder-- shit, fin. No damn pollution or whatever... What else was in that movie, hun?"

Her mom wouldn't answer; at least not for a few seconds. Finally, she would mumble, "I don't remember," into her phone screen. She sat hunched over in the corner of the room. Brooke always thought her mother was the one who looked frail under the fluorescent lights of the hospital room.

Peter turned from his wife to his daughter and squeezed her small hand. Then, he squeezed again. "I'm squeezing for mom, too," he whispered, smiling. His smiles, since the x-rays, became more and more apologetic. It wasn't his fault Brooke was here, but he always felt like it was. Maybe if he had done something different as she grew or during May's pregnancy; but he had become better at faking it throughout the years. He made as much progress as Brooke did.

Probably more, actually.

Brooke Kella really didn't see herself as Nemo.

First of all, Nemo was a boy. It shouldn't matter, but it did matter to a girl in elementary school. Nemo had his adventure with his father and his friends, and then lived happily ever after. The end. Brooke's "adventure", however, seemed never-ending. She was always stuck at the shitty part of the Disney movie, where all the progress she had made slowly fell apart. But, in the movies, there would be the next part, where everything gets as bad as it possibly can, and then she fixes it with a prince's kiss, or a round of archery, or sacrificing something for someone she loved.

It would get to a point, Brooke thought, where everything was as bad as it could get, and she would be ready. But she couldn't be ready if everything just kept getting worse.

"Your hair is thinning."

Dr. Chadwick had known Brooke from the first day she came in as a small child with a swollen shoulder and a sickly look. Even with such a history between them, the woman had nothing to say to the now small teenager. "But, it seems like - with the frequency of your chemo - thinning is the worst you'll get. You'll keep most of your hair."

Brooke swung her legs back and forth; a nervous habit of hers. They hit the wood of the examining bed with quiet thunks. Even though it was a nervous habit, the thumps had a rhythm.

"You're awfully quiet. I know you're tired, sweetheart. But you have to talk to me." Chadwick said sweetly, taking a step forward and a step down to look Brooke eye to eye. "How are you feeling?"

She held eye contact with her doctor for a few seconds, but looked away as she spoke, "I'm doing fine. Just lonely, is all. But that's nothing new, right?"

Chadwick scribbled something down. "I..." She tried to start speaking as she wrote, but paused until she was done. "I will tell your parents that. Maybe it will make your mom come and visit you more often, and maybe she could bring some family with her. I know you weren't too social at school, and I don't blame you. Immature teenagers are not good for socializing, and you're the exact opposite of immature," she spoke quickly, building into a rant. Brooke was used to it, and didn't mind. "Which is why you get along with adults so much more than you do with children your age, even though it is really good to be with kids your age because they understand you more. I'd move you to the adult wing if it wasn't so jam-packed and full of crazy people ranting about taxes and children who don't call and those weird insurance problems. I've always told your mother how lucky you are, how lucky she is, that you have good insurance. It'll be a big thing to get you through this. We're going to give you more chemo and have those ribs fixed up in no time, right, hun?"

"That's what they said last time." Brooke scoffed

despite her attempts not to sound critical.

"You know we're trying our best."

"But what if your best isn't good enough? I'd rather just die."

"Don't even joke about that." Her father's voice from the right corner made both Brooke and Mrs. Chadwick jump. It was the first time in a while Brooke heard him get stern so fast, especially since she began her treatment again.

Both of them expected something more from Brooke's father, but nothing followed. "Well, um," Dr. Chadwick started, "let's get you some rest then."

Brooke was then shuffled into her room, the vacant one that was long since shared. Even though it was vacant, Brooke and Peter both expected Mrs. May Boe to be in the room.

She was not.

Her daughter, however, was not surprised. Taking her spot in her bed, she rolled over to face the wall. Peter took this as a sign that his daughter wanted to sleep. He kissed her head and left to make a phone call, to his wife. God, where was she?

Brooke was alone. Her eyes popped open just to land on a crumpled, turquoise sticky note on a chair in the back of the room.

The light *tap-tap-tap* of her father's worn tennis shoes down the hall signaled her to climb out of bed and check what the crumpled piece of paper said.

"Needed my computer for a case. Be back in a bit. Love you - Mom.
P.S., tell your father that I'm getting him lunch."

The note was thrown into the nearby waste bin where it would stay. Lonely, Brooke had said. I'm lonely. And then they turned around and left her alone. Her only comforts now were the familiar room she had spent so long in and the stuffed Eeyore that her father fetched her from Disneyworld years before. She climbed into bed with her *stuffie* and hugged him tight. Sometimes, Brooke could hear Eeyore whispering things into her tiny ear.

"You'll get better."

Chapter Two

November 19th, 2012
2:22pm

"You'll get better. That's what I always told you. Was I right, or was I right?"

"Don't jinx it, you ass," Brooke hissed in a hushed voice as she smacked his arm.

"Besides, you hardly talked to me before this year. Don't run around saying you called it."

He laughed unashamedly, despite being in the middle of the teacher's lecture. No one in the room even turned their head though; Jace always talked too much. Especially when he sat next to Brooke in Pre-Calc. "I can't jinx it if it is already true. Unless I can... Do you really think I can? Then I might shut up. But only if you think I can jinx it. You know I'm not good at keeping my mouth shut."

"Shut up!" This time, it came out louder than she had intended. This time, people turned their heads. Brooke's light skin turned into the bright red that Jace was familiar with. "And you can," she said underneath her breath.

It was nice to see her cheeks light up; it meant she was healthy. Or healthier, at least. Jace only saw Brooke once a day in the winter semester, so, during that short time, he tried his best to light her cheeks up, to make her laugh, to make her slap him. She was something he missed so much during elementary school. Her energy was something he missed so much, something the chemo took from him. "Someone's getting attention from the class, hm?"

Brooke enjoyed his voice as much as he enjoyed nearly everything about her. His voice was very resonant. He could be whispering but everyone in the room would still hear him. Maybe that was because practically everyone was listening for him. Even the mention of his name made people look up from their phones or homework or comics or writing.

Jace Aiko Anderson.

"It is your fault." She pretended to be paying attention by scribbling doodles on her math notes. In actuality, she was looking at Jace. "Hey," she murmured during a break in the lecture, "when did we meet again?"

He just stared at her, stunned. "You're the one who told me this story."

"But you telling it is way more entertaining than me telling it, to be completely honest with you!"

"Wait, are you ever not completely honest with me?"

"Just remind me. Please?"

Jace knew she didn't want to pay attention to the class. He knew she liked hearing the story from him. He knew that even though their friendship was casual, there was a deep connection. Similar to a soulmate.

A soulmate of a friend.

Who needed everything to be romantic? Who needed everything to be alive and bright? Who needed everything to just be pretty or useful or smart? Why couldn't something or someone be all three? Friends were just as important as lovers, he thought, and usefulness was just as important as beauty or intelligence. That being said, he'd had a crush on her since they were in middle school. So at this point he was just preaching to whatever part of his heart thought he could get away with being just friends.

Brooke watched him space out. "Hey," she laughed, snapping her fingers in front of his face, "someone's going off into another world. I need you here, to distract me and tell me the story. Mainly the distracting part, I'm not a fan of Mr. Rivera's lessons." She always tried to slip her affection past him. She wanted to be casual. Unlike Jace, Brooke felt like everything had to be romantic or awkward. Her parents were awkward. Her friends in relationships switched back and forth between awkward and romantic like a light above a fascinated child's seat in an airplane, but they were never in the fuzzy spot in between. To Jace, that fuzzy part was where he was with her; just so happy without kissing her.

Happiness was what mattered most to him.

Brooke was always too worried about life to be worried about happiness.

Finally, Jace turned to her. "Fine, fine."

Chapter Three

May 8th, 2014
10:04am

He held a stuffed animal of Nemo the clownfish in his hands. He really wished he had found a bigger one, but this would do.

The little Nemo made Clara Barton Hospital look so much less intimidating. It was just like the ocean; full of odd things and odd people, full of life and death. Plus, it was a really tall building. He did not like heights. He had a particular dislike for hospitals in general. And he didn't know what he would stumble upon when he went into the daunting, cloudy, cancer-research center on the top floor.

He did know, however, that she wasn't dead. He would've heard about that. But the question was, was she at this hospital? Did she even want to see him? Would she be surrounded by other people? What if she was doing just fine on her own? What if she was on the very cusp of dying? The only thing he knew for sure was he asked too many questions in his mind and not enough out loud. This May 8th, 2014, would be the day Jace Aiko Anderson saw Brooke Kella Boe for the first time in ten months. His heart was pumping so fast, he felt like it might stop.

Or maybe it had already stopped.

"Hi," he croaked to the woman at the front desk.

Quickly he cleared his throat in an attempt to call his ringing voice back into his body. Jace knew he had a pretty voice. "Hi. I'm, um, looking for Kella. Shit, Brooke. Brooke Kella Boe, actually." It didn't help his nerves that the woman at the desk typed mindlessly at a computer. What could she possibly be typing? Many answers came to mind; diagnoses, apology letters to families, things he knew too much about and things he wished he could forget. He squeezed the little plush in his sweaty palms. *Shit, is she gonna be grossed out if this is sweaty? I should put it away.*

He shoved it in the pocket of his coat, and immediately regretted his decision. Now the stuffed animal was covered in sweat and crumbs from a granola bar from earlier.

It wasn't until Jace looked like he was panicking that the woman behind the desk finally looked up. She pulled at something close to her ear; a white cord. What? *Oh, headphones!* Now he felt stupid.

"Is there something I can do for you sir?" Her breath smelled heavily of an awkward sort of mint, like she ate an expired bin of chocolate mint ice cream or something weird like that. *Weird.*

"Yeah, actually. I'd like to see Brooke Kella Boe. She's being treated for Ewing Sarcoma here, I think. I mean, I hope she's here. It would kinda suck if she wasn't, I came kind of a long way. Not that I hope she's in the hospital! That would be rude and I want to be anything but rude to her like seriously she is wonderful and I-"

"One moment." Her jaw hung open lazily. *Click-click-click-clack-click* went the keyboard and a small doorbell noise told him she had found what he was looking for.

The next few seconds felt like they were a few months or a few years. "Here she is," the woman pointed to the screen, nail perfectly manicured. "She's available to visit in room 433. What's your name?"

"Jace Anderson."

Another strange look came to her face. Was it his name? Did she have some ex-boyfriend named Jace? That wasn't his fault, she shouldn't just run around judging every Jace on the planet. "Relation to the patient?"

"Um, family. No that's not true. Friends. Yeah, we're friends from school. I was hoping I could visit her here. Well not here, but, like, somewhere in the hospital. In the building or something. If she went home then that's fine but I've kinda missed her. I'm talking too much huh? Oops, heh, sorry. I'll just..."

An awkward silence followed. Jace was wondering if he was supposed to leave for the room or if he was supposed to wait for her to say something else.

"Room 433. You know," she started on some

story about having another Jace Anderson as a patient at Clara Barton hospital. "That was a weird case, it was..." When she looked up to the boy in front of the desk, he was gone.

He was practically running down the hallway until someone yelled at him. He tossed the stuffed animal up in the air and would catch it. This sudden glee had no valid source besides the wonderful little blonde girl he was about to see on the fourth floor.

Elevator, elevator, elevator. No elevator? Weird. Stairs work too.

He ran up the stairs two at a time, counting in Spanish in his head. It was an odd habit that his high school Spanish teacher had set him on.

Cuatro piso, cuatro piso, cuatro piso. Tres piso... *Cuatro piso!*

The large door wasn't so heavy in his state of ecstasy. He wondered what she looked like, if she looked any different. "She's probably still pretty," he said aloud this time. A surgeon flipping through a manilla folder was the only one to look up, though, and that made Jace feel slightly better about embarrassing himself in a public place. *Then again, that's what I used to be best at, right?* Now, he was making a mental effort to keep his words in his head. *She's always been pretty. She will always be pretty. I wonder if she still has those precalc notes I doodled that one thing on it. It was a bug or something. No, that would be weird, right? For her to keep them would be weird. I doodle on everything. I really need to stop carrying around sharpies, it's becoming a problem. A really weird problem.*

Room 433. Or was it four twenty two? No, four thirty three was definitely it.

Fourth floor. Room thirty three.

Four.

Three.

Three.

Four hundred and thirty three.

He reached for the door handle slowly, like it might disappear if he grabbed it too fast or if he blinked. In the back of his mind, Jace thought about how stupid he must've looked in the hallway. The door handle glided down under the pressure of his bony hand, and the door was a lot heavier this time. Then, it fell open. Light from the window reflected onto the floor and back up into Jace's dull eyes but he continued to move forward into the room. The first person he saw was not Brooke, however; it was her father, Mr. Peter Boe.

"Um, excuse me." Jace's expectations of a blonde teenage girl were drastically wrong as he came face to face with a middle aged man with balding hair. "Sorry, am I-"

"Oh, are you a new nurse or something?"

Jace tried to formulate a sentence but it all came out as some mix of English and Spanish. He stopped himself, took a breath, and let it out. "I'm here to see Kella. Shit, Brooke. Brooke. I'm here to see Brooke. I was a friend from school about a year ago, in her precalc class, and I just heard she was in the hospital. I mean, in here."

"Jason? What are you doing here?" Brooke's tiny voice rang from the right side of the room. She was still in bed, hugging her Eeyore, but she suddenly sat up and began to straighten out what was left of her hair. Most of her hair remained; however, it was stringy and gross and made her more self-conscious than almost anything. Her mom always got mad at her for that. "You have bone cancer," she would always say, "I can't believe you're worried about your hair. Don't worry about your hair, worry about your health."

Peter extended his hand to Jace. "Jason? Always nice to meet a friend of Brooke's! I really, actually appreciate how you took some time out to come out here."

Wait. Is he talking to me? Was she talking about me? Hold up. Jace frantically scanned the hospital room for another male. What if Brooke had a boyfriend? *That would be so bad.* He calmed down when there was no attractive, male body in the room. Including his own.

"Y-yeah," he shook Peter's hand, "nice to meet you, sir."

Brooke was unusually quiet. Well, not unusually quiet. Brooke was pretty shy in school, but she was too silent in the context of the situation. She just sat in the corner brushing her hair down into place. She was phasing out, as Jace would like to say. Daydreaming. But did Brooke Kella Boe really forget his name? He tried his best not to look offended because it wasn't polite to correct them right now.

Peter took Brooke's silence as her wanting him to leave the room. "Well, uh, I'll let you say hi to her. Leave you two to talk and... Whatever."

Jace now realized who Brooke inherited her shy, quiet attitude from. Not necessarily awkward, though. Jace was awkward. Brooke and Peter definitely were not. They had filters, at least, and didn't trip over their feet on a regular basis.

Peter took two long strides past Jace and out of the room. From what Brooke could tell, he was going to get coffee. Maybe that's where her mother was as well, but Brooke wouldn't have been surprised if May Sanderson Boe had just went home instead of bringing food to Peter as she promised.

"Jason, I haven't seen you in, like, six months. Eight months, maybe? We weren't even friends outside of class. What are you... Why?"

"It's been ten months," he casually corrected her. Jace shoved his hands into his pockets and leaned on the doorframe, faking a good amount of confidence. "Well," he rubbed his chin thoughtfully, "maybe you weren't friends with a guy named Jason outside of class, but I'm pretty sure that I waved at you whenever I saw you."

Silence.

"And I think I carried your books one time."

Confusion.

Understanding.

Understanding was not followed by panic. Well, at least not visual panic. "I'm really, really sorry. Honest." There was audible panic, it seemed. *Great, the first person to visit me in weeks and I screw up his name. Maybe I should tell him to leave now, before I mess up anything else.*

"It's okay!" He laughed. He couldn't help but laugh. He was happy to see her and she seemed decently amused to see him. "It is fine, really, I promise. Don't worry about it." Inside, though, it hurt him a little. Her name stuck in his head like someone had carved it into the inside of his eyelids. He thought he was being good about hiding his hurt feelings, despite the doubtful look on Brooke's face.

It was a long time before Brooke finally

demurred, "It's not fine, it was mean of me. You've been in my classes since, what, kindergarten?"

Forcing himself to drop it, he rolled his eyes. "Aren't you at least happy to see me? I came all this way to say hi. So, uh, hi. Hello. I can say hi in, like, three different languages if you want. I could say it in binary!"

Now Brooke was finally starting to realize; her classmate from precalc over a year ago came all the way to the hospital to say hi to her. Did he secretly want something from her? Panic rushed over her features and turned her face red. Jace couldn't help but notice, and just assumed she was flattered.

"Someone is a little blushy today, hm?"

He contained his slight disappointment. Her cheeks were not as bright as they had once been. Jace took this time to look her over; the dull hospital gown, her pale skin, her thinning hair, her skinny wrists. The only bright things that remained as he remembered were her eyes. Her beautiful, bright eyes. Her bright blue eyes created a dramatic contrast between her exterior and interior. It was then when Jace realized she was not too far gone. It was then when he realized she would live.

"Shut up." Brooke made an extra effort to move across the room to smack his arm. The light reflected off of something in the corner of the room, and an orange flash caught the corner of her eye. "What's this?" She barely mouthed it while she picked up the stuffed Nemo. "Did you, uh, bring this, Jace? It isn't mine."

"Oh!" A nervous laugh escaped him, "Right. I must've dropped it when I walked in. Yeah, it was for you, actually. So, it's yours now. Take it. I figured you would be lonely. I mean, that makes it sound like you don't have any friends. Wow, shit. That's not what I was saying at all, I know you have friends. I just meant I didn't want you to be lonely and it was on sale on my way here and just take it I'll be on my way." Wow. *That went downhill so fast,* he thought, *I didn't even have time to try and brake. It was like tripping on the stairs to heaven and instead falling back to Earth. Does that mean she's my heaven? Wait, no, that's creepy. Now I have that one Radiohead song stuck in my head. Yeah, I should go.* His thought process delayed him by approximately two minutes. After those long two minutes, he finally turned on his heel to head back into the rainy atmosphere.

During his thought process, Brooke was allotted two minutes to respond. Considering all factors, this was a decent amount of time for her to say what she thought about the stuffed fish in her hands. Two minutes was not enough.

Two minutes and hearing his two footsteps was enough.

"Wait."

Chapter Four

"Wait, are you telling me that you couldn't be there after my surgery because you had a party to go to?"

"It was thrown in my honor! I couldn't just not show up!"

"You could've said you appreciated it then left! They would've been happy that you weren't there to consume all of the damn campaganeh!"

"Brooke, it is pronounced *sham-pain*. *Champagne*. And I couldn't leave, your father couldn't pick me up."

"And why couldn't you drive yourself?"

"I had a couple of glasses."

"Of what?"

"Champagne, alright?! I'm sorry, I'm sorry, I'm sorry! Stop blaming me for your cancer!"

Silence.

Peter internally screamed from the corner. Then, he actually screamed and his hands flew up into the air.

"Can we just drop it? I'm sorry, I shouldn't have even said anything."

Brooke wanted to say it wasn't his fault. She loved her father. She loved her father with all her heart. But her mother, since the treatment started, managed to fall downhill faster than Brooke's health did.

May took a seat at the kitchen table. "You're damn right you shouldn't. It wasn't any of your business."

Any of our business?

Are you kidding me?

The father and his daughter were stunned into silence. Peter was fearful for his daughter's feelings, slightly concerned she would punch a wall, and Brooke was just utterly repulsed. "Any of our business? You told me you had an important case to work on!"

"I'm the one who worked so we could pay to get you that surgery! You know what? I'm not discussing this with you two anymore. I'm done arguing." May Sanderson Boe stood as quickly as she had sat. She strolled out, followed by the sounds of the expensive two-inch heels click-clacking against their stained wood floors.

Brooke's disdain for heels grew from that event, from her mother's occupation. She stormed up the stairs, wishing she could scream but instead keeping it to a whisper. Upsetting her father now wouldn't help herself or him. "I shouldn't be surprised, but I am. I'm *repulsed*. But she lies for a living, what else could I expect from her?"

Repulsion with the human mind.

Repulsion with lawyers.

Repulsion with drinkers and campaganeh or whatever it was. Champagne.

None of these were truly justified, Brooke knew in her heart, but it didn't matter. If she wasn't cancer free, if they found another tumor, she was dead. She could do whatever she wanted if she had another Ewing tumor. Brooke went to bed with one ill wish that night.

And someone, somewhere, made it come true.

Somewhere downstairs, Peter wondered why they had to have a teenage girl with cancer and a lawyer mother. Triple the drama he needed in his life was already caused by his family. "Jesus," he muttered as he set his head on the table, "I need a god damn vacation."

Chapter Five

May 8th, 2014
10:09am

"You really... Bought me this?"

Brooke tossed Nemo between her bony hands, keeping her eyes down towards it. "Didn't just dig it out of the trash can or anything? He's... Covered in crumbs. And he is... Kinda, uh, wet too." *Well, it is cloudy outside.* For a moment, she had a nice thought of Jace coming down from the clouds to visit her humble little hospital room.

"I really bought it for you. But, I mean, I kinda lied. Not off of a sale rack, I lied about that, oops. Full price. Totally worth it, though."

That's a dumb thing to lie about, she thought. "You know, you're as weird as I remember you being," Brooke spoke clearly, so he would hear, and threw her arms around his torso for a nice hug. Jace was always ridiculously tall and it was never fair.

He was tall and skinny and smart and she wasn't any of those things. Well, now she was skinny, but it wasn't by choice.

Jace felt time slow drastically the second she touched his deep green jacket. In slow motion, she came at him. How long had he waited and how far had he traveled to hold her for the first time? Slowly, he reconciled the hug. His chin positioned itself on her head.

"I thought you were done growing in tenth grade," Brooke teased. His arms pulled her close and a warmth flowed from him into her. Later, when she had the words, she would describe it as a warm glow in her back and chest. Almost like life, flowing from him to her.

"I thought you were done with this whole cancer bullshit," Jace replied. "But here I am. Here we are, I guess."

Brooke had opened her mouth to make another comment before his 'joke' shut her down. The space between their voices grew into one of awkward, uncomfortable silence.

An awkward chuckle finally came from her mouth. "How'd you know I was here?" Brooke's arms dropped to her sides with an uncomfortable noise of her hospital gown shuffling. "There are other hospitals around town, you know." The stuffed Nemo caught her attention again. She fluffed it between her hands, brushing crumbs off of it and examining it. It was an attempt to bring a light heartedness to the room.

"Just a lucky guess. I guess you could say," Jace prepared his comment with a dumb smirk, "a little fishy told me."

"Jesus, Jace. Did you come all this way just to tell

me a bad joke?"

"No."

"What'd you come for, then?"

"To tell you a *great* joke. Plus, Nemo needed a home. I couldn't take him with that dog I've got, he wouldn't last a week." Gently, he took the stuffed fish from her hands. Nemo then took a spot on the bed next to roughed up Eeyore. "That Ewing shit won't stand a chance against two Disney stuffed characters."

Brooke balled up her fists, grumbling, "You don't always have to be talking about my disease. Actually, it would be great if we never talked about it. Please, just tell me about other stuff. Tell me how your summer was. How was graduation? I haven't seen you for a really long time, I need updates. Wait a second. Isn't it a Tuesday? Why the hell aren't you in school?" She became more enthusiastic as she spoke to him. "I'm always open to visit, but not if you're missing school. I will call security and make them make you go to school, I promise."

Jace laughed half heartedly. "Funny story, about school." Plopping down on the empty bed with a sigh, he grabbed Eeyore and squeezed him. *Him, he's fluffy.* "Uh…" Now he was distracted. *Fluffy fluffy fluff.* "Uh… Oh! Did I ever tell you about my mom when we were in class together?"

"Uh, no." It wasn't a complete lie. Brooke knew

Ms. Dianne Anderson's situation because she eavesdropped. Eavesdropping, as she would never admit it, was one of her favorite things to do. Her mother yelled at her for it as a child but apparently it never stopped Brooke from doing it in high school. "I don't think you ever told me." She was also a bad liar.

"Well," he continued with a straight face even though he knew she was lying, "she divorced my dad when I was, like, ten. It started when I was eight. They started acting all weird around each other, and dad would randomly take me out of the house to run away from her to go see a movie or something... Anyway, she was low on money for a while but then she wanted to get married again to this guy, Sam, recently so I dropped out to get a job to pay off the wedding debt. That was back in, uh, January. Uh, December. The wedding was in January. Besides, college was a pain in the ass anyway." *Fluffy fluffy fluff.* "I didn't fit in very well."

For a moment, Jace began to think about his father. Eight years flew by so fast that he felt like his father was just around yesterday. Despite the surprisingly clean divorce that tore his parents apart, Jace loved his father. He was his hero. He had a motorcycle and was so unbelievably loyal. Aiko Ken Anderson's favorite hobby was retrieving lost baseball caps from the bottom of the lake where he worked. Then, he would hang them up in their garage. *Why did they get divorced in the first place? I can't remember.*

"You? Not fitting in? I'm gonna call bull. Sorry,

Jace. It's just not possible." Brooke chuckled, poking his cheek. It brought him back down from the clouds. From the cold, dark clouds to the warm, white sheets of the hospital bed. Jace was one of the most charming people Brooke had ever met, in his own awkward, ranting sort of way.

He wouldn't hurt a fly - unless he accidentally fell on it or something. He couldn't be held accountable for his lanky limbs.

Jace smiled, but only because she smiled. "So, yeah. No school, just work. Lots of work. Too much work. How was your summer, Brooke? All I saw were Facebook updates from Aaron, and *someone* got a boyfriend."

A modest laugh came from Brooke. "No, no." She really was just too embarrassed to talk about it. It was like when you think about something too much, a break up or a date, and pick apart everything that went wrong until the point it drives you entirely mad.

"Yes, yes," Jace bounced up and down on the bed, chanting, "yes. Yes yes yes."

"Sorta. You've got it all wrong, really."

"You're stalling. Just tell me the story already!"

C h a p t e r   S i x

"Just tell me the story already!"

Brooke had been practically begging all period. Well, maybe not begging. But she certainly wasn't happy when he would say no, and she would look back to her precalc; something she was good at.

Jace couldn't comprehend how any normal human being could be good at math. But, seeing as science was going to be his major in college - and that involved math - he was so screwed. "Ask her to tutor you!" his friends pestered. His mom said that a lot too.

"Fine, fine. So, we were in precalc. And I didn't know anyone in this whole class, because it's all Juniors."

"Cuz you're not good at math."

"Thanks for reminding me. Do you want to hear the story or not?"

With that, Brooke shut her mouth. Her chin was propped against her hand, and she drummed a soft beat against the desk with a forest green pen. She always seemed so... relaxed. Laid back. But Brooke was just really good at keeping her stress hidden.

"So..." Jace took a moment to locate his train of thought. "The teacher said we had to partner up for an assignment. And I was like, well, shit." He glanced to her face, and - seeing her look of great amusement - he smirked. "Then we partnered up, and I was weird and you were weird and here we are. Is that good enough for you?"

Brooke smacked his arm with the back of her hand, "Not even close. You're an awful story teller."

"See, this is why we don't hang out outside of pre-calculus; you hit me all the time!"

"Really?" She struggled for something snarky to say back.

After a few moments of her silence, Jace stuck his tongue out at her. He then threw a charming grin and turned back to his notes. His notes were littered with little doodles here and there; music notes, mushrooms, masks, bugs, books, song lyrics, poems, movie quotes, band logos, you name it. They were interesting in contrast to Brooke's, as hers were incredibly... Organized. Jace called them organized because he thought it would be too mean to call them boring. Really, her page was practically blank besides the notes. Not even highlights or different colored pens or anything like that.

All she had drawn was a small clown fish in pencil in the top right hand corner.

Nemo.

C h a p t e r S e v e n

May 8th, 2014
10:19am

"Nemo? How did you know that my dad…" Brooke lost her train of thought while she examined the little toy.

"You probably told me once or twice, you staller. Tell the story to Nemo, pretend I'm not here." Jace took the Nemo and held it in front of his face. "*Tell me the story about your boyfriend, Brooooke.*"

His ridiculous attempt at a Nemo voice seemed to break her. "Fine, fine." Her laughs quickly took on a more nervous tone. "I, uh, I was at this party. It was like this, um, honors precalc party to celebrate the year ending and everything. You weren't there, I guess because you had graduation that night or whatever. But it was a pool party and I didn't know it was a pool party." Brooke actually looked at the Nemo while she spun her tale. "And that asshole, Travis, you remember that guy? He used to sit behind us and be a jerk to practically everyone in the class. But he, uh, picked me up and threw me in the pool in my clothes, and I can't..."

"You can't swim, right." Jace made little Nemo nod.

"Right." *How does he know that? Did I tell him?* "So Travis threw me in the pool... And, uh, remember

Aaron?" Aaron Lambrinidis was probably one of the prettiest boys on the entire high school campus. He was a little immature, though, and desperately wanted to be popular when he was in middle school. In high school, after puberty dealt him a good hand with those striking eyes and perfect hair, he relished in the attention he received.

"Oh!" He suddenly began bouncing up and down in his own excitement. "Did he save you or something? I always called that he liked you and you never ever believed me! Did we ever bet? Do you owe me money? I think you owe me money even if we didn't bet."

"Shut up," she brushed her hair back behind her ear. "Uh, sorta. He dove in, wrapped me up in a blanket and brought me home. He asked me out on a date a couple days later."

Jace was so irresistibly smug. "I think you owe me money. I recall making a bet about that Aaron kid."

"Nope. It didn't last past a few dates."

"Why not?"

Just a shrug from her.

"What kind of answer is that?" He pushed her shoulder playfully, then recoiled. "Shit, sorry." Jace pulled his hands back and squeezed the Nemo. He muttered under his breath, "um, here," awkwardly placing the stuffed animal against her 'bad wing' and then put it in her hands.

Jace had always been so touchy about touching her right shoulder. He just felt awful because he didn't know how else to feel.

Brooke was just mad because everyone thought it was their own fault. It wasn't anyone's fault. But that didn't mean she wasn't appreciative of people's thoughts when it came to sincerity. Fighting with her words, she tried her best to comfort him. "No, don't worry about it."

Then, it was quiet.

Quiet.

Quiet.

Quiet enough to hear a pin drop.

Quiet enough for Jace to hear his heartbeat ring in his chest and throughout the rest of his body, down to his big feet and his big hands.

Quiet enough to make Jace say something.

Not quiet enough to make Jace think about what he was saying.

"Where's the cancer now?" Again, his voice came out crinkled and dented. He didn't make an attempt to clear his voice and ask again though. He was just desperate for the answer.

Quiet.

Quiet.

"My ribs. But I'm getting another scan... I might have some in my legs now..."
"Good thing I brought Nemo, then, huh! Disney Stuffed Animal Therapy - apply one stuffed animal to each infected area. You'll be good as new in no time. And then we'll go to Disneyland or something. After you make up your senior ye-"

"No."

No?

"My survival rate drops... drastically if they find malignant tumors in multiple areas." Brooke had heard this repeated to her too many times. The vernacular continuously floated through her veins.

"I'm back, Nemo."

Peter walked into the hospital room, three cups of coffee precariously balanced in his two hands. "I got a decaf for you, black for me, and I just got Jason black but I brought some creamer."

Brooke forced a shamefaced smile. She took the cup but did not drink, instead she just used it to warm her hands. Rain tapped against the glass like the fingertips of impatient patients long passed.

"Thank you, Mr. Boe, I really appreciate it." A polite and also very poorly told lie.

She knew he hated coffee.

"Hun," Peter took a sip of his coffee, then smiled, "you have a couple more appointments today. Could, uh, Jason maybe come back some other time?"

"Yes! I mean, I could definitely come back tomorrow. If you want. Brooke probably needs her rest and stuff, right? If you guys want me to come back tomorrow. But, uh, yeah. I'll get out of your guys' hair and come back tomorrow. I don't have to."

Lonely, Brooke's mind screamed. She had said she was lonely.

But now, she didn't stop him from leaving.

Jace shook her father's hand, hugged Brooke, grabbed his coffee cup and was on his way.

"Talkative, that one, and judicious," Peter murmured. "Where'd he come from?"

"Honors precalc class in my junior year. But we never… Really talked outside of class. Never even exchanged numbers or anything. Oh, and his name is Jace... I kinda messed it up."

"Hm," Mr. Boe nodded, stroking his daughter's hair. "Some of the best friends are like that, though. You don't know how much they care for you until they're already gone. And I'm sure he was glad to know you remembered him, even if it was all a little fuzzy." He kissed her head and trailed off. "I don't know where your mother ran off to. It's getting late."

"Dad?"

"Yeah?"

Mom's probably at home, drinking. No, that would hurt him too much. "Um… What does judicious mean?" She faked a smile, but it ended up looking too sheepish.

Peter decided not ask what his daughter was thinking. If there was something on her mind, she would tell him when she thought it was best. "Judicious means… Having good sense. Good intentions, I guess. I think he's pretty nice, and I hope he hangs around here some more. We need something to laugh at besides me." Chuckling, he wrapped his arm around her shoulders.

"You and me both," Brooke murmured with a very small smile.

Chapter Eight

May 8th, 2014
10:19pm

Jace Aiko Anderson didn't go home that afternoon. He decided that he had two options; sitting in the stairwell, or sitting in a waiting room somewhere. Sitting in her hall would be way too creepy. But all of the waiting rooms were closer to the bottom of the building, so Jace picked sitting in the stairwell between floors Three and Four.

Now, he was happy to have some coffee; it would keep his hands warm for a little while. He made the assumption that there were no heaters anywhere among the staircases. Nemo wasn't in his pocket anymore. *I know she needs it more, but now I'm lonely. At least there's decent wifi in here!* In his pocket, though, was a little iPod with some headphones. They were a labyrinth of a tangled mess, but Jace had all of the time in the world.

His golden voice really went to good use then. It echoed, bouncing off of the walls as he sang the cute little song about an old couple, living together in an old house. Sure, he wasn't the best at hitting the notes, but most would call it decent singing. *Tap-tap-tap.* Jace kept track of the beat with his feet.

And that was where Jace Aiko Anderson spent most of the afternoon, and all of the night of May 8th, 2014. A stair was his pillow; his jacket was his blanket.

Sleep definitely didn't come easily. But it was all so, so tremendously worth it.

Because now, he could be closer to Brooke Kella Boe.

He didn't know, however, that while he slept that night, Brooke had a dream. An important - albeit short - dream. She could not remember a lot of it afterwards, but one image stuck with her;

Jace Aiko Anderson with a golden halo.

Chapter Nine

September 17th, 2007
8:36pm

Brooke didn't regret missing most of elementary school. Sure, she lost out on some of the social skills developed by the other kids, but she was way further ahead academically. And she never felt like she fit in at Casimir Pulaski Elementary anyway.

Her missing time made her feel like nothing mattered.

Nothing mattered. Not in a negative sense, though, not like life was pointless. People's opinions of her literally meant nothing. Her opinions of other people literally meant nothing. As far as Brooke was concerned, they were kids who were lucky enough to get educations. That's what her father always told her.

"I didn't get to finish high school," Peter told her when she was young.

"Is that why mom has a job and you don't?"

His daughter's intelligence surprised him sometimes. *Then again, she is her mother's daughter.* "I guess so. But I *really* don't have a job because I like being around here, with you. Who's gonna burn your grilled cheese sandwiches every day if it's not me, huh?" His pale freckled face lit up with the fun-loving smile that had always comforted Brooke over the years.

With a laugh from his daughter, Peter scooped up her up and threw her over his shoulder. "You're heavier than a sack of potatoes, you know that? Jeez. I won't be able to carry you around much longer, Nemo."

They went past May on the family computer. May pretended not to see her husband and her daughter having so much fun while she had so much work. Perhaps, Brooke realized upon hindsight, that was why her mother was so bitter. Bitter like the glass of champagne sitting next to the keyboard.

Peter let Brooke down in her room. "Bedtime, Nemo."

"But I'm not sleepy! I wanna catch fireflies, Dad."

"Nope. You have your first day of fifth grade tomorrow, you gotta get your beauty sleep. We can catch fireflies during the weekend." Peter kissed Brooke's forehead. "Don't forget to brush your teeth, alright?"

Brooke nodded but continued to pout. At this age, she had thick, light blonde, slightly wavy hair, which came from Peter, not May. She bounded off to bed with her stuffed Eeyore; a bag of candy corn hidden beneath her bed.

Peter could not contain the glee he felt from being around his daughter. *I made that. How did I ever get so lucky?*

"You shouldn't be encouraging her not to finish high school."

May dramatically spun around in her swirly work chair, glass in her hand. "I heard you talking, you know."

"No wonder she eavesdrops... I'm not encouraging her. But she should know that she has the right to make her own decisions. She's much smarter than you give her credit for, which is kinda dumb because she got being smart from you. God knows I'm not the smart one." Peter sat down on the couch across from his wife. *Snarky* would easily be the best word to describe Peter's attitude. It came with good cause, though; May's lack of attention since Brooke's cancer treatment meant it was up to Peter to balance the scales. "I'm not the smartest guy," he started, looking at his feet, "but I know when you have a kid in need, you pay *more* attention to them. Not less."

Only silence met his statement; silence from the black-haired beauty in the corner of the room. All she did was sip her champagne.

After a few moments, Peter stood and left the room. He went outside and sat on the driveway, looking up to the stars for the words his wife could not find.

Chapter Ten

May 9th, 2014
9:00am

"Day two! Alright. Hopefully, I'll get longer than twenty minutes with her." Jace was as excited as a small child seeing a spaceship in person. He hopped up the stairs - two at a time as always, but stopped right before he got out of the stairwell.

Should I get her something? No. That would be weird. Right? But most people bring flowers for people in the hospital. Would it be rude if I didn't bring some coffee for her dad or something? Or some breakfast? No. No no no no no no no no no. Jace, don't make this weird... But it what if she thinks I'm rude? Then I came all the way down here for nothing. Okay, fine. Some flowers. But I really can't go overboard.

He ran back down the stairs but only one at a time this time. If he had a dollar for every time he had fallen down a large staircase, he would have enough money to take Brooke to Disneyworld. And if Jace had two dollars for every time he had fallen and ate shit on concrete, he could pay for a hotel for two days. Hell, maybe three.

Flower shop. Gotta find a flower shop. Or a coffee shop, whichever comes first. How much money do I even have? I'll worry about it later.

A Ralph's was the first thing he came across. Its

bright red sign was dulled slightly by the dark of the early sunrise and the dreary clouds scattered across the sky. It looked like it might rain again today.

Jace made a trek across the street, through the parking lot, and into the Ralph's. Upon entering, he spotted the perfect yellow roses brushed with slightly red - tinted tips. To his right was a Starbucks.

They're both in one place? Okay, don't panic. I'll just get some coffee for Peter and flowers for Brooke! But her mom might be there. Shit. Okay, tea, coffee, roses. In that order. How do I even know her mom likes tea? It's the thought that counts. Jace abruptly changed directions from going to the little flower booth to the Starbucks. He ordered a black coffee and some hot tea. While he waited for the lackadaisical "barista" or whatever, Jace grabbed the bouquet of yellow red-tipped roses that seemed to be patiently waiting for him. The white bud in his ear played some fitting music for his frantic, excited run.

Roses? Check. Tea? Check. Coffee? Check. A way to carry them all? Check! Through the bitter cold and the really, really hot coffee, Jace made it back to the hospital.

Meanwhile, room 433 was still in eight in the morning on a Wednesday mode. Peter slept slumped over in a chair in the corner. Over the last months, he had configured quite an impressive little sleeping area out of chairs, blankets and pillows.

43

May sat in a chair close by, on her phone. She wasn't doing anything even remotely important. It was Peter's fault that Candy Crush was installed on her iPhone.

Jace Aiko Anderson couldn't have made a noisier commotion if he tried. He came crashing down through the doorway. The roses, clenched between his teeth, fell out of his own fear of the thorns slicing his mouth. The coffee and tea were salvaged though, as he managed to keep them upright through his glorious entrance. "Oops," he grumbled. A slight groan of pain followed.

The smack of the grown eighteen year old's body hitting the white, tiled floor was enough to wake Peter up. May dropped her phone. Brooke walked in after breakfast and nearly tripped over his body.

"Jace? What did you- How did you- I... Do you want any help?" She was already taking the cups from him and setting them on a table by the time she got her words out.

Jace pushed himself up. "Thanks. Jesus, that floor hurts. I hope I didn't make a dent or anything. But I wouldn't be surprised if I did, to be completely honest with you... I should probably, uh, explain. I wanted to bring you something but I was worried that I should've brought your dad something then I was worried that your mom would be there so I got something for all of you but I didn't know how to carry it. So, uh, here. I got you some roses, I got your dad some coffee, and your mom some tea." He looked around the room frantically for the drinks. They sat on the nightstand by Brooke's bed. Swiping them up, he carried them across the room.

Peter, in a sleep-induced half-coma, took his drink and almost dropped it. "Thanks, Jason..."

May's phone rested on the floor, screen down. Getting angry was her first instinct. Her second instinct was being upset. Her third instinct was calming down, and doing nothing for a few seconds. Luckily for everyone else in the room, she decided to opt for the third option. "Oh, thank you. Your name's Jason?" May took the tea absentmindedly and stared at her phone. She was worried that when she picked it up, it would be shattered; just like Jace's confidence.

Jace just assumed she couldn't lean over to pick it up herself, so he picked it up. "Here you go. Sorry, I didn't mean to come crashing down in here. I just wanted to be nice. Oops, shit!" A crunch beneath his sneaker made him scramble to the floor once more. The roses had been scattered out along the floor with some losing petals and thorns. Jace attempted to gather them all together and put them back into the plastic wrap they came in. "Do I need a vase? I should've bought a vase, huh? I can go get that. Just hold these for a sec."

"Jace, Jace!" Brooke couldn't take his panicked rambling anymore. Not that she didn't identify with or understand it; she just didn't want him to panic unnecessarily. She gently set her hands against his chest. That same light glow seemed to touch her heart.

"Don't worry about it, 'kay?"

He took in a deep breath. "Okay. Sorry, sorry. Seriously, take them. I just thought they were pretty." This time, he tried not to shove the roses at her, rather offered them.

Brooke took one hand off his chest to take the bouquet of flowers but left the other hand on his chest. "They are pretty…" The roses had such a refreshing scent compared to the stale, sick air of the cancer research center. "Um, do you want to go walk around; outside maybe?"

Something about her voice seemed…*off* to Jace. No, not her voice. But there was something different. Then he remembered what she said yesterday, about having another scan for Ewing Sarcoma in her legs. His eyes went wide and Brooke noticed.

"Hey." She snapped her fingers in front of his face. "Come back down." Jace seemed to disappear when he daydreamed. He went up into the clouds and sometimes forgot how to get back down. That, she claimed, was the reason he wasn't good at math.

"Huh? Oh, yeah, sure. Let's go. You should lead the way."

"Are you sure, hun?" Peter asked sleepily from the corner. "It's pretty chilly out there. I don't want you getting a cold. Might rain soon, too."

"I'm sure, Dad. Don't worry about me." Brooke gently pulled Jace out of the room.

"Jeez," she laughed, "I feel like I never get away from them sometimes. I love them, but..."

"I get it," Jace muttered. He began taking off his jacket.

"Jace, it is gonna be cold."

"I know, but you're the one in the thin hospital gown. At least I've got some layers."

Then, Jace Aiko Anderson wrapped Brooke Kella Boe up in his deep green, almost black jacket, and up into his arms bridal style. "Shall we use the stairs or the elevator? I couldn't find the elevator yesterday. I'm convinced it doesn't really exist. How do they get wheelchairs up to the second floor? Magic, probably. I knew hospitals were spooky." For a moment, Brooke felt like he might drop her, but he was just readjusting his grip. One hand rested on her back, the other cradled her legs.

Brooke made an odd noise around the lines of a squeal. "Jace! You're an idiot." She smacked his chest, laughing.

As far as Jace was concerned, though, the important thing was that she didn't ask to be put down. After she called him an idiot, he began to grin like one. "So, what'll it be? I would personally recommend the elevator, if it exists, just because of the fiasco where I tripped. I'd rather not drop you."

"I think I'd prefer that too, so go with the elevator."

"Alright!" With a nod, he started down the hall.

Brooke knew he was going the wrong way but she decided to keep it to herself. She could not, however, restrain herself from smirking slightly. Jace wasn't looking down so he didn't notice. He arrived at the end of the hall, and suddenly looked similar to a lost puppy.

"I know there's an elevator somewhere. I saw it, I think. Right? They wouldn't have a hospital without an elevator. Unless they would… I'm losing my mind. Probably because I have a concussion from your floor. So should we use the stairs?"

She was just so amused when he rambled. Was it because he was nervous? Or did he just have a lot on his mind? He didn't seem to have a filter, either. Jace was this strange, otherworldly creature to Brooke. Extroverted, goofy, nervous, tall, lanky, and full of bright colors. An alien. "The elevator's on the other end of the hall, Jace." Brooke giggled. She poked his cheek, then pointed in the right direction. "You're not losing your mind."

"I'm not?"

"You can't lose what you don't have."

"Aw, that was mean! Here I was, thinking you were trying to be nice." Jace's lips slid into a pout. "It's probably true, but still pretty mean. Pretty cruel."

"Probably? Definitely. You're insane."

"Maybe you should be nicer to the guy who gave you a jacket and is carrying you down four stories."

"Maybe it doesn't count because I didn't ask you to do any of those things."

"Oh, yes you did."

"Did I?"

"Nemo told me that you didn't feel like walking. I trust Nemo. Nemo's always honest and always nice. Unlike someone I know," Jace rolled his eyes with a teasing tone in his golden voice. He loved teasing her so, very much.

"Maybe I shouldn't tell Nemo so much, then."

Chapter Eleven

August 11th, 2012
11:06

"I can't believe her!"

"I know you're mad, hun. But..."

"But what? It was completely irresponsible of her to sit there drinking campaganeh or whatever while I was getting half of my scapula removed. It's damn ridiculous," Brooke practically had steam spitting out of her ears. After the argument with her mother, Peter went up to check on her. He had hoped that she'd gone to bed, or was on her computer, or doing homework, or anything but dwelling on what happened so many years ago.

"But..." Peter took time to chose his words carefully. "She's your mother," he sighed, "and she loves you. She just...isn't sure how to handle stuff like this, you know? She's much more mathematical and calculating and... Confusing, sometimes. That's where you get your math skills. Lord knows I'm not good at math."

"That doesn't give her any right to be awful to me or awful to you. Nobody has any excuse to be awful to anybody!" Brooke clenched and unclenched her fist. She bit her lip. *No, don't ask. It might make him mad.* "Why did you even marry her anyway?" Brooke regretted it immediately and returned back to biting her lip in anxiety.

Quiet.

Quiet.

Silence.

Peter grew up believing he was the very definition of the stereotype of the middle child. He was the middle of five children, and he was the only one who wasn't adopted. He was also the only one who did not play a sport, the only one who did not finish high school and the only one who didn't get laid by the time he was sixteen.

He grew up believing he was the most ordinary child on this side of the Mississippi River. Why the Mississippi River? Good question, his mother likes to use that expression as a hyperbole. His mom was pretty normal and his dad was pretty average too. They were all pretty average but Peter felt like he was average times a billion. His name might have well just been John Smith.

In retaliation to his normalcy, he dropped out of high school. This would be a decision he would regret soon after, and for most of his life up until he had his daughter, Brooke Kella Boe.

But yeah, he dropped out of high school and started caddying at the local golf course. He lived up near Harvard law school. "Three generations of Boes," his father would rant, "living in this house. And you will all fight to the death for it, right guys?"

The other four boys would laugh, albeit a little confused. Peter shook his head in a teenager-y rebellious manner. "I'm gonna move somewhere far away and marry me a pretty girl and I'll go further than all of you in life!"

"You won't if you don't improve your grammar," his oldest brother retaliated. They all laughed.

His second day of caddying was the first day that Peter Christopher Boe met May Stephanie Sanderson.

Peter Boe remembered it so well.

A sigh.

"Well... I met her during one of my summer jobs. It was... Four years after my junior year of high school. I was caddying, and she was in her first year at Harvard Law. The teacher treated some of his best students to a free eighteen holes, and I happened to be caddying that day for your mom. And I... I just thought she was the most beautiful person that I had ever seen. And she must've thought I was pretty nice, because she gave me her address. We wrote to each other for... a couple of years, probably - it was all so long ago. We finally met again after she was done with her degree, and she moved in with me. She was - well, she still is -

so beautiful and intelligent and she always knew what she wanted and wasn't afraid to go after it. But she...she has always been difficult. Or, complicated, I suppose." Peter began to daydream about what life was like back then; the cheap wine on apartment floors with pizza, cuddling with his then-girlfriend while she was surrounded by law textbooks. He knew if he didn't return to the ground, he would be lost in his mind for days.

"Anyway, could you please, please give her a break? Her parents weren't as forgiving as mine and she grew up in a totally different situation than you or me. She's just worried and stressed out with her job. She loves you more than you know. Please; I know what she did wasn't right, but she truly, honestly just wants what's best for you, okay?" Peter blinked a few times to get himself out of his memories, even though that's where he wanted to stay. But Brooke needed him here. "Go to bed." He kissed her forehead as usual. "Unless... You want me to bring you some Oreos or something."

By this point, Brooke's head rested on her father's shoulder. "I guess that makes sense... I don't want her to act like that, though."

"I don't think you can't change that, hun."

Only quiet contemplation from Brooke. Her lips pursed into a funny shape as she thought, and stared off into the deep blue of her walls. When she was young, her parents painted the room like an ocean. The whole 'Nemo' nickname was never created to stick; it was just a joke, a way for Peter to comfort his sick daughter. But when May was in a good mood, she loved it. Their whole house evolved into having a sort of oceanic theme. They weren't even close to the beach. In fact, Brooke had only been to a beach once or twice. "If I can't change that... Can I have some Oreos?"

"Of course, Nemo. C'mon downstairs with me. Maybe Mom's calmed down a little."

She removed her head from his shoulder and started down the steep staircase with him. Before they started down the staircase, Brooke read the little typographic poster that sat just above the light switch.

"Oh shut up. Every time it rains, it stops raining. Every time you hurt, you heal. After darkness, there is always light and you get reminded of this every morning but still you choose to believe that the night will last forever. Nothing lasts forever. Not the good or the bad. So you might as well smile while you're here."

It still made her smile. Cheesy and cliche, but happy.

"Oh," her father practically jumped, "I've been meaning to ask you. What happened with that nice Andrew kid?"

"His name's Aaron. I haven't heard from him in a while, actually." The last time he acknowledged her existence was after a date when he posted a picture of the two of them in front of the movie theater. Jace Aiko Anderson liked it on Facebook, and she wondered constantly how smug he must've looked. Brooke thought about Jace much more than she would admit or even realize.

"That's a shame. Maybe he just couldn't handle how pretty you were."

"Dad, c'mon."

"I'm serious! It took me years to finally say anything to your mom. Pretty girls are like boys' Kryptonite."

Brooke honestly, seriously thought it was because of her scar. There was a large scar along her right shoulder where part of her scapula had been removed. The last date she was on, she made the mistake of wearing a strapless dress. He didn't want to put his arm around her. He didn't want to sit on her right side. She wanted to just think Aaron was squeamish, but... it was hard to not be self-conscious about the scar. Her dad, her mom, even her doctor always insisted it was part of her.

"It's what makes you Nemo," assured her Dad. "Your lucky fin."

"It's something that has shaped your childhood and will most likely continue to shape the rest of your life. And your body is nothing to ever be ashamed of." Doctor Chadwick.

"It doesn't matter," countered Mom. "Don't

worry about it."

Either way, it shouldn't have mattered to Aaron. It shouldn't have mattered to anyone. It shouldn't have mattered to her. But she just wanted it to go away. She didn't want a bad wing, or a confusing mom, or a weird, blotchy face, or bony fingers.

Sometimes, she just didn't want to exist. Sometimes, it was most of the time.

Chapter Twelve

May 9th, 2014
9:41am

The garden was not Brooke's favorite spot on the Clara Barton Hospital grounds. In fact, it was pretty far down on the list. Whoever tended to it must've either died or went on a two year vacation to the Bahamas, but either way, all of the plants were dying. None of them were indigenous to the rainy area and usually needed more sunlight to thrive.

"Wow. This is a little... anticlimactic."

"Yeah. Sorry. Even the cafeteria looks better than this place."

"But it's probably good for you to get fresh air sometimes."

"I have a window."

"You're so introverted."

"You're so annoying; I swear to God. Damn extroverts with your talking and your fresh air."

Jace just scoffed. It wasn't raining, luckily, but it looked like it might start soon. They took a seat up against a hospital wall, overlooking the city streets.

Looking at the city just reminded Brooke of

everything she missed. When she was younger and was between treatments, she had a Yorkie puppy named Maddy. Maddy passed away of old age shortly before her sophomore year, but during the precious time they had together, Brooke grew closer to her than she had to most other human beings. Truthfully, Brooke didn't like humans.

Jace loved humans. And dogs, but humans too. Most everyone loves dogs so it's not a big statement to say that somebody does. He used to have a big golden retriever named Pooh Bear and the world's smallest Siamese cat named Sally. When he slept alone, especially in stairwells of hospitals and in hospital rooms, he missed Sally. And it gave him a little comfort to think Sally probably missed him too. She was the world's smallest - and probably most affectionate - cat.

Anyway, what Brooke missed. Brooke missed school. Brooke missed amusement parks. Brooke missed libraries. Brooke missed movie theaters. Brooke missed real food. Brooke missed junk food. Brooke missed Netflix. Brooke missed her junior English teacher. Brooke did not miss her sophomore or freshman English teachers. Crazy walnuts, they were. Or are. Probably still as insane as they used to be. Brooke missed watching movies when it was cold. She missed hot drinks that didn't taste like powder and water.

She used to miss Jace.

Now she just missed him when she slept, and

she couldn't sleep when it was cold.

"Uh," Jace was hesitant to interrupt her thoughts, "someone looks like she's deep in thought. Whatcha thinkin' about?"

Brooke decided not to answer for a few moments. Her eyes smoothly rolled from the cityscape before them to Jace's chest, his collar, then his face. "Thinking? I'm thinking about... Things."

"Things. That narrows it down a ton."

Quiet.

Jace was constantly longing to say things he could never say to her. None of them were really that dramatic, either. No Nicholas Sparks love confessions or Edgar Allen Poe poetry recitations, just... He wanted to make her happy. And not just happy for, like, three seconds. Sure, that was really nice, but not what he really wanted. He wanted - no, needed - to make her happy and healthy and meaningful. Or maybe she was the only one who could make herself feel that way. Jace just really, really, really, really wanted to help. Really wanted to help.

She didn't know yet, but he was helping.

His arm rested on the back of the bench, like an eighth grader trying to make his move on a first date at the movies or something. Childish, really. But Brooke liked that; it was refreshing. She was always expected to be so mature and everything. Sometimes it felt like she had to grow up too fast.

"What are you doing, Jace?"

Jumping nearly three inches, Jace sucked in so much air that he almost began to choke. "What? Nothing. I'm just resting my arm. That's not a crime, right? Unless it is. In that case, I've been breaking the law for a couple of years. I should probably start running then. Nice to see you, though!"

"Jace, you talk too much and you know exactly what I meant."

Brooke, knowing Jace was so much like a child, treated him like he was an adult when he needed to be.

Someone finally expected something of him.

"I was just… Gonna… Uh. Do this."

Chapter Thirteen

April 18th, 2013
8:13am

"Prom was… Awful. Junior prom was just awkward, but there is no other way to describe my senior prom other than awful. Horrific, maybe. No, that's too dramatic. Um… Dreadful, maybe.

"I shouldn't have gone with my ex. Remember Courtney? That was my first, and probably most fatal, mistake. We hadn't broken up too long ago, and it was just a small breakup. I thought, maybe, we could try to be friends. I thought she was really nice and sweet and stuff. Plus, she helped me out with a lot of my history homework. I really shouldn't have taken AP econ. I know you told me that, and you have every right to say I told you so.

"Anyway… I was thinking too much right before."

"And probably talking too much, but go on."

"Right. Anyway, I don't know why I started dating her, really."

"I know why you started dating her." Jace's mom looked smug as he told his story the morning after prom. Her new boyfriend, Sam, tried to pretend he wasn't eavesdropping from the kitchen. He wasn't very good at it.

"Mom, that's gross."

"No! Never mind, I'll explain later. You dumb teenage boys. Get your head out of the gutter."

"Jesus, stop interrupting. I picked her up from her house and everything was suddenly a bazillion times more awkward than it ever had been before."

"God, you're so bad at math."

"What did I tell you? She admitted something to me on the way there. Courtney never really liked me that much either. She was using me. Well, sorta. But she was trying to figure out what was going on with her and her ex, when I came along. I guess I was just a distraction. She apologized and I... Didn't mind that much, actually. I didn't mind that she used me. It was really weird. I wanted to be mad. I really, really, really wanted to be mad. But I wasn't. I was sorta... Relieved.

"Yeah, the rest of the night sucked. She ditched me for her ex and they were actually crowned king and queen. At the end of the dance, I was dateless, dance-less, my shoe was messed up, and my clip-on bow tie wouldn't clip back on."

His mother listened intently, taking a sip from her coffee cup every few minutes. "Yeah, but," she spoke softly when he was done, "that sounds like a pretty average day for you, don't you think? It wasn't horrific or whatever word you used. Your junior prom when you were kissing a girl when one of your rubber bands for your braces caught on one of her brackets. That was so much worse. I had to get a pair of scissors to get you guys apart."

"Dreadful. I called it dreadful. And thanks for reminding me. But it was awful! It was terrible. It wasn't even that terrible. It was really normal and not soap opera worthy and I know it. But I just…"

"You wanna know why you thought it was awful?" Dianne asked. She loved being a mother for almost this exact reason: teaching. Except this was a little bit of sassy teaching. "Remember that girl from your math class? Brooke, I think."

"Brooke Kella Boe," Jace nodded, "what about her?"

"You hated it so much because she wasn't there with you. You dated Courtney because you didn't want to admit that you wanted to ask Brooke to prom. You even know her full name, Jace. You recite it a lot. It's a little weird."

"What's your point?"

"Just ask her out already."

Chapter Fourteen

May 9th, 2014
9:58am

Instead of Jace Aiko Anderson's hand coming down lovingly on Brooke's shoulder, he poked her. "Tag!" His mischievous tone was followed by him darting off the bench and into a muddy, grassy field between them and the road.

"What? No. Don't start this."

"Too late!"

"No! We'll get in trouble."

"I thought I had you figured out, Brooke Kella Boe. I thought you wouldn't back down from a tag game if it meant your life. Guess I was wrong..."

Brooke was so ridiculously, unreasonably irritated with him. And that made her want to kick his ass into the ground with a game of tag.

Jace saw the look in her eyes and realized the mistake he made.

It was the calm before the storm; she looked down, removing her slippers. Then, she pulled her hair back into a ponytail. The air took on a different mood when Jace could see the pale, bald spots on her head. Brooke bolted towards Jace with a ridiculous amount of energy. "I don't turn down a game of tag!" She laughed, chasing him with her arms out.

"See, that's the Brooke I know! C'mon, fight me!"

"You're ridiculous!"

"You're the one chasing me barefooted. That jacket looks like a cape on you. You're practically the new disney supervillain."

Circles and circles and circles were carved into the grass by their feet. Brooke actually enjoyed the feeling of the mud, the grass in between her toes. She felt like she was catching fireflies with her father again, before her cancer.

Jace felt like he was flying. That is, until he fell hands- and face-first into the mud. Actually, he flew into the mud. "Ugh, ouch." He didn't realize what happened until he was on the ground. But at the same time he didn't mind that much.

Brooke, on the other hand, could see her downfall coming from miles away. Time slowed down just as she tripped over Jace's abnormally and disproportionately large feet. He did break her fall though. Only her hands hit the mud, but her face was spared by his back. "Ow."

And, just to prove its point, the universe decided to make it rain right at that exact moment. It could've started ten minutes earlier, ten minutes later. *No*, Jace thought, *the universe hates me and it feels the need to prove it to me every second of every day.*

"You okay?" Jace started to turn over, so he could see her.

Her face - covered in mud, rain, sweat, hair, whatever - was somewhat of a shock to him. To have her that incredibly close. His thumb brushed her cheek, leaving a smear of mud.

"Oh, now you're starting a mud fight? Real mature." Brooke retaliated with a full hand of mud to his nose.

"What? No! It was on accident, but if you really want to…"

"No, no. The nurses will throw a fit."

"Oh, okay."

Quiet.

Quiet.

Quiet.

If this was a cheesy Disney Channel movie, I would kiss her. But that would mean there would be a part of the movie where everything goes downhill and sucks for a while. I don't want that to happen. No, don't kiss her. This is only your second day visiting her anyway. And you're covered in mud. She might take away points for being romantic.

After Jace's mental soliloquy, he sat up. She was now in his lap, and was still wearing his jacket.

She sneezed.

"Shit, you're gonna get a cold and it'll be my fault." Jace didn't really mean to say that out loud but he did. He just felt really bad about it. Hastily, he scooped her up and carried her back inside.

Their muddy bodies were a wonderful change compared to the rest of the research center. Wonderful maybe wouldn't be the word that the janitor would use, but it was definitely Jace's choice word. Brooke's choice word was something along a muddled sneeze or sniffle. God, she got sick so fast and so quick. Her parents would hate him. He could almost see his whole plan fly out the window.

"You're really warm." Brooke's nose was pressed against the blue fabric of his button up shirt. The glow returned again. Maybe he was just made of light. Maybe he was like a dog, made out of sunshine and happiness. It would definitely make sense. "It's nice..."

"I think you're really cold. Sorry, that was a stupid idea, huh?"

Brooke stopped him, cut him off mid sentence. She could just feel a rant coming. "No, no. Don't worry about it. That was the most fun I've had in a while."

The elevator doors opened to the fourth floor hallway, and Peter was right outside. He had been heading down to find the couple, but Jace just figured this was more of the world hating him. He wanted to help her clean up before giving her back to her father but now he would definitely be kicked out of room four hundred and thirty three forever. "I, uh… We… Sorry. But, um, we were playing tag and I tripped and she tripped and now I think she has a cold. I'm really really really really sorry. Really. I'll put her in her room and then leave, I promise."

"Whoa, slow down there, Jason."

"It's Jace."

"Jace, right. Slow down Jace. You guys were playing tag?"

"Yeah. Was that bad? I didn't think it was bad. I'm sorry!"

"Just, uh… Bring her back to the room. I'll go get something warm for her to drink." Peter shuffled past Jace awkwardly, not wanting to get the mud and grass and dirt and rain and sweat and whatever else on his jacket.

Jace didn't notice his awkward demeanor. He instead just wandered down the hall and listened to Brooke's directions to get back to her room. A kind, blotchy-faced nurse waiting in the room took Brooke from him, took off the jacket, and led her to go wash up. Jace wanted to go with so badly. *Wow, am I really clingy? Shit. Well, that's not my biggest problem right now.*

Brooke wasn't surprised when she looked inside her room and noticed her mother was nowhere to be seen. It only dampened her spirits slightly, as a dumb grin much like Jace's regular expression graced her face.

Now Jace could finally relax. He went into the men's bathroom, cleaned up, and came back into the hospital room. Adjacent to Brooke's bed was another bed, empty and just begging for someone to sleep in it. Preferably, someone who slept with a concrete stair as a pillow last night.

No, I shouldn't. No, don't. Sleep in a chair. Be a normal visitor. What if they need that bed? Aw, screw it, they can just get me up. Wow, this is nice… I missed beds. Beds are so nice. It's like… A cloud… A squishy, fluffy fluff cloud.

Peter was sort of surprised to see Jace sleeping in the empty bed, but he also wasn't too surprised. Little did Jace know that Peter caught Jace sleeping in the stairwell. Peter didn't like to tell his daughter or his wife, but he knew that the stairwell between the second and third floors didn't have a fire alarm, so every night he would sneak away for a single cigarette. He almost tripped over Jace on his way down.

Despite the fact that Peter could have actually died from tripping over Jace's unconscious, lanky body, he was really happy. He was really happy that someone was there for his daughter. Someone gave two shits. Peter gave way more than two shits and had the feeling that Jace did too, but Peter felt like sometimes Brooke didn't feel loved.

"You're obligated to love me," she half joked once, "you're obligated to call me beautiful and feed me and stuff like that. But I don't know if I could actually… Talk to anyone. It's been so long since I talked to someone who didn't have a job here or who wasn't related to me by blood or marriage. What if I can't talk to anyone?"

"You'll do fine," he told her. "Everyone loves you. And if they don't, fuck 'em. Oh, shit, don't tell your mom I said that. She doesn't like me cursing around you."

So Peter took his seat in his little fortress in the corner. Lulled to sleep by the soft rain, the smell of the outdoors from Jace and the clearness of the air, Peter passed out.

Brooke came in to see the only two people she enjoyed interacting with sleeping. She decided that meant she could sleep too. Now, she had to decide where to sleep; Jace's comforting warmth or her own bed where there was an absolute zero chance of anyone getting mad at her or looking at her funny.

Eh, fuck 'em.

Chapter Fifteen

May 29th, 2014
9:06am

"You're doing…" Dr. Chadwick flipped through Brooke Boe's paperwork, "really well."

"That pause was really convincing."

"No, I mean it! I mean, in the last twenty days since we found the tumor in your left leg and the other on another rib, you're doing remarkably well. And even with your cold two weeks ago, I thought that would set you back pretty far."

"Yeah, maybe it wasn't the best idea."

Peter sat against the left wall, ecstatic. "That's great! Really, that's… Fantastic. Unbelievable. Do you think she'll get out soon? Maybe the cancer is subsiding. Then you could go back to school, Nemo!"

Brooke tried her hardest to conceal her thoughtful look. Didn't this always happen in the movies? The person seemed to be getting better, but it was really the body's last kick against the door before falling over into a six foot grave. Four weeks ago, that was exactly what she wanted. She just wanted to die peacefully. The only thing truly stopping her then was her father. It sounded selfish to say but he truly didn't have anything, or anyone else.

But now, she wished and wished with all of her heart to stay alive. She wanted to reverse what she had wished for before. It was like there was some cruel, asshole genie somewhere who enjoyed toying with her health and taking her wishes too literally or not literally enough.

Her appointment wrapped itself up quickly and Brooke was left inside her lonely room. Every bump and crack and flick of discolored paint was engraved into her mind. Peter told her when she was little that she started naming the tiles in her old room. Half of them were named Erica. Erica was her favorite name. She asked multiple times to change her name to Erica Brooke Boe.

"Why get rid of Kella?" May would ask. "It was my mother's name." Her mother that she hated but her mother nonetheless. Her mother was solely responsible for funding May through Harvard Law school. Brooke was happy that she never had to meet Kella Sanderson.

"I don't like it. People always think that it's Kelly."

"Just tell them that they're wrong and they can go stick their nose in mustard!"

Peter liked to say that for no reason at all.

But her middle name now just reminded her of Jace and a conversation on one of the first couple of days of precalculus.

"Brooke Boe?" The terribly under- qualified honors precalculus teacher looked up from his clipboard. Mr. Rivera would always be remembered by Brooke as one of the strangest men she had ever met and would ever meet in her lifetime. And that included Jace.

During role call, there was no response from the class. "Brooke, uh. Kelly Boe?"

"It's Kella," she politely corrected.

Jace sat on her right side. His eyebrow practically jumped up his forehead. "Your middle name is Kella? Not Kelly?"

"Yep. It's Kella."

"No way."

"What?"

"I've gone the majority of my life believing it was Kelly. It's gotta be Kelly."

"Or maybe you were just wrong for once." Brooke hadn't been in the mood for the sassy kid who sat next to her in precalc. She woke up on the wrong side of the bed, and just couldn't stop thinking about her mom's obsession with campagen. *Champagne*, she corrected herself. *If I'm gonna argue, I gotta sound smart.*

Jace was more than a surprised by Brooke's snark. As far as he had known, she was the quietest girl on this side of the school. She did no harm but she also took no shit, from anyone, apparently. "Brooke Kella. Brooke Kella Boe. I'm gonna remember that, I promise."

"Yeah," Brooke grumbled without bothering to look up, "right."

"I will! I'll call you when we're both, like, fifty or sixty and just shout your full name into the phone."

Every day, when he saw her, he would call her by her full name. He would greet her this way and say goodbye as well. This was the very beginning of their little flirty half-friendship. They didn't talk outside of class. They never exchanged numbers. They never went to each other's houses. They did add each other on Facebook, though. That was one of Jace's friend's faults.

So why was Jace so positively, absolutely, one thousand and one percent in love with Brooke Kella Boe? Well, maybe not in love. He didn't like to say he was in love with her. It felt a little creepy if she didn't know about it, and it felt even worse when he dated Courtney.

C h a p t e r   S i x t e e n

May 30th, 2014
9:00am

Jace had a set routine when visiting Brooke in Clara Barton Hospital, which was slightly unusual. Jace wasn't one for routines ever, not even in high school. *Especially* not in high school. He wasn't good at studying or planning or organizing or anything vaguely of the sort. But maybe because it involved Brooke, he was making more of an effort.

Every morning, he brought roses. It became a force of habit, even though Brooke was running out of places to put them. The roses were always either yellow with red tips, or light blue, or sometimes a purple because it was her favorite color. He brought a cup of coffee for Peter but stopped bringing tea for May, because she was hardly there when he would visit.

After he bought the roses and the coffee, he picked up a newspaper for Peter. This made him arrive at Clara Barton Hospital around nine in the morning, since he was still sleeping in the staircase. Except now, he had taken a pillow from an open supply closet in the middle of the night. He kinda felt bad, but not too bad.

He greeted the woman who worked at the desk, even if she still looked at him kinda funny.

He ran up the stairs, two at a time.

Room four hundred and thirty three.

Four.

Three.

Three.

And over the time he visited Brooke, he too began to memorize every bump and crack in the whole building. Well, at least in the stairwell and room four hundred and thirty three. And the elevator... And the garden where his face imprint still remained in the mud because it hadn't rained since. But he didn't name the bumps and cracks Erica, like Brooke did. He named them after Disney characters like the incredible dorky dork nerd face that he is, was and always would be.

The big crack on the step between the first and second floors was named Quasimodo. The smaller crack near it was named Esmeralda and he named the railing Phoebus. *Is that a weird thing to do?* He never named anything Nemo, though, because his one and only Nemo was up in froom four hundred and thirty three. *Now that was weird. I'm calling a girl who's not my girlfriend by a pet name. A fish name. Does that make it fishy? Pfft. That was really dumb. Good one. Tell that one to Brooke and she might hit you in the face.*

His ridiculous pun made him stumble on the fifth to last stair from the door to the fourth floor. Luckily, only his chest and legs pounded into the concrete and he managed to save the black coffee and purple flowers. But then, he began to slide. As he began to slide down the concrete steps like a child down a slip- n- slide, he contemplated the nice life he had and wondered what his funeral was like.

"Jace! Jesus, get up!"

Brooke interrupted his reminiscing when she emerged from the door at the top of the stairs. Only a few minutes before had she been wondering where Jace was. She knew he didn't like schedules, but also knew he was bothered if he wasn't there by 9:15 in the morning. And she missed him. She missed him a lot. She missed him in her sleep and when she ate breakfast. She missed him when he walked out of the room. There was just this warmth that flowed from him that she enjoyed so much, and had never found in another human being. Brooke believed she had her own little glow but also believed it was well complimented by Jace's glow. It was like blue and red mixing to make a light and gorgeous purple.

Jace probably would've jumped three feet in the air and fallen on his face if he wasn't already eating the concrete. Instead, he just twitched in surprise. The hot coffee was spilled on the stairs, but he still kept a tight grip on the roses. He held on so tight, the thorns were piercing the plastic and starting to enter his hand. "Oh, hey, Brooke! I just… Wanted to see what the staircase looked like from down here. It's a totally different perspective." He liked teasing himself. "I mean, that was after I fell, but you gotta be optimistic, you know?"

A graceful giggle came from her slightly chapped lips. "You're ridiculous."

His heart melted with her giggle and he struggled to keep his composure. "You say that a lot. Maybe that should just be my nickname," he laughed as she helped him up, "The Adventures of Nemo and Ridiculous! Causing problems at a hospital near you."

"I can't believe you wanted to go into science. You would've been a great entertainer. It's so much fun to watch you make a fool out of yourself."

Jace took a goofy bow and handed her the purple flowers. "Oh yeah? Here, I can go up to the hallway and slide around in my socks if it would make you laugh."

"It probably would make me laugh... I'd love to watch. But you say that like you wouldn't do it by choice in the first place!"

"I'll do it on one condition."

"I pick you up afterwards? Because I don't know if I can promise that. You're giant."

"You have to slide around with me."

"I don't have socks."

"You don't have socks? You're kidding me.

There's gotta be a pair of socks somewhere in this building. If you can find weird things like defibrillators... Defieblaters?... Defiblablabas or whatever, and syringes, pokey things, you should be able to find socks." In his enthusiasm, he pointed an adventurous finger up towards the stairwell door. "Onward, Nemo! We have trouble to cause."

"But..." Defibs, or defibrillators, and syringes were really normal in hospitals. They were probably more normal there than any other type of place on earth. Arguing with him won't get me anywhere. "Alright, Ridiculous. You're so weird." *Oh god. I can't call him that. Dad would think it was ridiculous.* Brooke made herself laugh but didn't say anything else during their travels to her room.

Like a true gentleman, Jace Aiko Anderson held the door open for his beloved. She followed through the doorway with a quiet thank you in his general direction.

On this particular Sunday morning, the hospital seemed to be at peace with the rest of the world. The thing that Brooke hated most about living in these white walls were the days when everyone was hurting. Everyone was in and out of the hospital, someone got diagnosed with cancer, someone lost a baby, someone was in a car accident. And there were the people crying as well; their wife of twenty years diagnosed with ovarian cancer, a mother whose daughter lost her own child, the mother and step-father to be of a boy who passed away on the way to a wedding. Hospitals, on most mornings, seemed to be like graveyards.

But today she began to think about all of the babies born, all of the tumors removed, all of the broken bones mended. Because Jace was like her cast on a broken arm. Sure, she could've fixed herself without him, and she had help from her family, but Jace being there really was the icing on the cake. And she never knew how to thank him.

Jace walked with his hand lightly placed on her side as he usually did. Brooke had become so used to the bright glow radiating from him that it just naturally brought a smile to her face.

Sure, they weren't an official thing. "Official schmofficial," Peter liked to say, "that boy looks at you like you're the sun and moon and grass and everything he's ever given two shits about in the world."

"Dad, that's the biggest cliché I've ever heard."

"But you can't tell me it's not true, can you?"

Anyway, back to Nemo and Ridiculous.

"So, are you gonna slide around on the hallway tiles or what? I can go get some popcorn probably."

"Not until Nemo finds some socks. If you can find popcorn, you can find socks."

Their playful banter felt like it was rudely

interrupted, when really, they were just shocked to see May Sanderson Boe sitting in room four hundred and thirty three without a cup of tea or her phone.

Chapter Seventeen

May 30th, 2014
10:36am

She was just sitting there, waiting for the two of them. Well, probably just Brooke, but Jace felt just as threatened if not more so.

Brooke pulled Jace's hand away from her side, and stepped in front of him. She held his hand behind her back.

God, he admired her so much. She was scared and angry but she still stood up for herself. She was so brave.

"Hey, Mom."

"Hey sweetie. How are you feeling?"

...What? Who is this woman and what has she done with my mother? "I... Uh, good, I guess? What are you doing here? I thought you had a big case today or something like that."

May hadn't been in hospital room four hundred and thirty three for a couple of days. Brooke had been counting; it had been five since the last time she saw her mother and her father in the same room together. *Maybe she left,* Brooke wondered, *maybe she finally lost it.* The more she thought of that possibility, the angrier she became, so she tried to soothe herself by squeezing Jace's hand.

"Well... I lost. But that's okay, it was just a civil case anyway. Dr. Chadwick called me and said we needed to talk. Jace, honey, could you just sit here for a little while? Peter's waiting for us in the office."

Brooke's heart stopped, turning into an empty metal hollow. She was going to die.

Jace wasn't entirely sure what was going on but when she dropped his hand, he knew it wasn't good. "I... Uh, yeah. I can stay here." Stepping past Brooke, he grabbed the stuffed Nemo off of her bed and handed it to her. "He'll make sure you're alright, okay?"

"Okay," Brooke choked out. The metal traveled from her heart up through her vocal cords. She felt as though her soul was already beginning to leave her body.

And just like that, May took Brooke Kella Boe away from the icing on her cake to go see what was going on. Brooke Kella Boe was taken from the man, the boy, the whatever who looked at her like she was the moon and grass.

Then he was alone. Lonely.

"Crap. What am I going to do? I have to do something. Eeyore, what the hell am I supposed to do?"

Eeyore didn't respond for him like he did for

Brooke. He just stared into Jace's eyes with the same unknowing look that Jace had on his own face. "Eeyore, you're really not helping me out here."

The toy just stared.

"Should I tell her? Nope. No. No, no, no, no, no, no, I can't. That's not advisable by any standards. Not yet, at least."

Years and years and years went by before Brooke, May and Peter came back into room four hundred and thirty three. Jace was just lying on his back on the floor, even though there were two open beds in the room. The floor just felt like a much more fitting place at the moment. In his right ear was his dirty, plastic earbud playing music into his mind. It was a nice, instrumental piece from the *Finding Nemo* soundtrack. *I liked it before I met her,* he would insist to himself, *it's not weird or anything.* Besides, James Newton Howard was the shit when he was in high school. *Plus, I've always been a big Disney fan.*

Jace began to think about his father, and his parent's divorce. God, where had he even gone? He just fell off the face of the Earth when the last custody form was signed and faxed to the court.

Chapter Eighteen

September 17th, 2007
12:11pm

Aiko Anderson did not fight for custody of his only child. He always said he was a lover and not a fighter.

"I want a divorce," Dianne told him as she packed her things. "I can't handle you taking Jace away on your motorcycle and whatever else you do. He can't grow up like that."

"Okay."

"A-and, you're not helping at all with the house or even raising him."

"I know."

Why the hell did he do that? Why did he act like he couldn't be bothered to give two shits about his wife or his son? Why was it so irresistibly charming? Dianne knew it was dangerous the moment she met him in the American South while an older Bing Crosby song played over the speakers of the nice restaurant.

"I'm tired of taking care of you. You still act like you did when we were kids, and Jace can't look up to you."

"I understand."

She didn't say anything to her husband of fifteen years. "You're absolutely ridiculous. You can't even pretend like you care, even for your son?"

Jace picked up his cursing from his mother. He sat during this particular argument with his ear to the closet door, where he had been hiding.

But really, Aiko cared.

Aiko Ken Anderson cared so ridiculously much about his wife and his son and the life they built together in this small house in this small town in this small world. He had nothing before he met Dianne West. But she always knew what was best for her and he always respected it. Aiko had a curse he would later call 'caring too much.'

Jace did not understand that, though. Not until he was much older and it was too late.

Dianne West was out of the house within minutes of their talk, or of their one-sided conversation. She had a roller suitcase in the back of her minivan, and she let Jace sit up in the front seat.

And that was when Jace knew something was up. Mom only let him sit in the front when something really good was happening, or something really bad was happening. He hoped with all of his heart it was the former, but the packed bags in the back told him otherwise.

The silence killed him.

His mother turned on the radio, only to be greeted by some Bing Crosby song. Now, Jace had grown up with that Bing Crosby. It was Bing Crosby when his parents sang loudly and off key in the living room on Sunday nights when the wine bottle was empty and cheap pizza sat on the kitchen table, when there was laundry to be done and cares to be had and damns to be given. Dianne and Aiko really didn't worry about any of that.

Jace heard Crosby singing and took it as a sign of everything being alright. So with his little, golden voice, he sang with it. "Let me call you sweethea-"

The music shut off with an abrupt click from the stereo system. Tears were pooling in Dianne West's eyes. She never, never wanted to hear that song again. It reminded her too much of Aiko... But so did Jace. Jace, the little half-Japanese boy who sat in the car with her, who inherited almost everything from his father.

Well, except the grace. Jace picked up from Dianne's clumsy side of the family that always stubbed their big Irish toes on walls and couches.

"Mom, why'd you turn it off?"

**

Jace's train of thought was interrupted by Brooke

and Peter reentering the room. May was nowhere to be seen, and Peter stepped back out of the room to leave Brooke and Jace alone. There were tears in her eyes.

ChapterNineteen

May 30th, 2014
10:38am

"Brooke?"

His blonde friend stood in the doorway of the room, her bright eyes cast down. Her eyes were so much brighter than the rest of her being and Jace loved it. He strongly believed that the eyes were the window to the soul. That's why he always believed his eyes remained a dull, greenish grey.

Her eyes, however, had tears pooled around them. Brooke finally dragged her eyes up to meet Jace's. "U-uh… Remember how I told you they were saying how I was doing really good?"

"Yeah, why? You have been doing really good. You've always been really good. You're really good. I mean, as a person. Is that weird?" Jace began to panic and he wasn't good at hiding it. His words became faster and faster and prevented her from talking. Maybe I could prevent her from saying whatever she was going to say. Maybe I could just stay in this moment where we stand together and just talk, maybe I could stay here forever if she doesn't finish her sentence. "You're great. You've always been great."

"Jace."

"Yeah?"

"Calm down."

"That's really easier said than done, you know."

"I know. But just... Try. Here. Hold Eeyore." Brooke handed him the fluffy stuffed cartoon character. She realized she had to comfort Jace when Brooke was the one delivered bad news - but it didn't surprise her that much. Brooke took care of Jace just as much as he took care of her, probably more. Make that definitely more.

"Okay..." Jace took the stuffed animal in his arms. He hugged it close to his chest and took a deep breath through the nose, and let it out through his mouth. "What about you being good? With your cancer."

"Um... I've been doing really good. But Dr. Chadwick thinks it's just... It's the last stretch."

Silence.

His brow jumped in confusion. "The last stretch? You mean before you're better for good, or..."

Jace knew what she meant. Brooke knew that Jace knew what she meant. And Brooke wished just as much she didn't have to tell him. Brooke choked softly, "You know what I'm saying."

His jaw dropped to protest, then he quickly

clamped it shut.

Silence.

The rain came down lightly outside and the noise resonated through the room. Jace, for a moment, thought about how his face imprint in the garden would be erased and reformed in the mud.

"You're not going to die, Brooke."

"That's bullshit, and you know it."

"You're not going to die, I promise."

Another moment passed and Jace rushed forward to hug her. He wrapped her up in his arms and sat down, holding her close. "You're not going to die."

Even in this immense moment of disbelief, of fear, of sadness, Brooke Kella Boe could still feel his glow mixing with her own. It was such a familiar, comforting feeling. She felt it in her shoulder, in her rib, in her leg, like the glow was fighting off her cancer. It was something she wished she could harness into a drink or a food. But she couldn't do that, so she just kept Jace close instead.

"How could you possibly know that?"

"I just do, okay? Trust me. You're not going to die. Not from this Ewing bullshit. You've got two

Disney stuffed animals and a big clumsy idiot to fight off that shit, and we are going to do a damn good job."

Brooke said nothing. Jace felt her tears begin to soak into his shirt.

"I know for a fact you're not going to die."

"Stop lying."

The rain became heavier. How fitting, Jace thought, for such a melancholy moment. Brooke knew this moment would come, as did Jace, but that didn't stop them from wanting to be anywhere else in the world.

Her words felt almost physically wounding. She thought he was lying. "I would never lie to you."

"Then stop it."

In Jace's disbelief, he became frustrated. "I'm not lying to you, Brooke Kella Boe. I could never lie to you and I never have lied to you and I never will lie to you." That itself was a lie. But soon, Brooke would know all of the truth. And by soon, he meant eventually.

Brooke knew even that was a lie. "So," she continued, wiping at her nose with her sleeve, "my parents are thinking about taking me home. There's nothing they can do for me here... Besides chemo. I want to stay and do chemo, though."

"Why?"

"If I'm going to die... I want to go out fighting."

"You're not going to die, I swear to God."

Chapter Twenty

May 30th, 2014
6:00pm

When Peter wanted to leave Jace and his little
Nemo alone, he signed papers to let Jace stay overnight.
Jace Aiko Anderson was now registered in Clara Barton
Hospital records as a member of the Boe family. He
could visit whenever he wanted to, and didn't have to
sleep in the stairwell anymore.

*Should I tell Brooke about how he slept in the
stairwell? Nah, she'd feel bad.* He began his trek back
up four flights of stairs to his daughter's room. Peter
liked walking, it gave him time to think, and it gave
Brooke and Jace more time alone.

Brooke was alone. Alone with Jace.

Lonely, she had said.

During an appointment, Dr. Chadwick met Jace
by accident; he opened the wrong door, thinking it was
the bathroom. After the tall, dark haired man left,
Brooke's doctor smiled. "Is that Jace?"

"Yeah. He's a little..."

"High-maintenance?"

Brooke couldn't help but laugh as a blush graced
her face. "Not exactly. He just doesn't think things

through sometimes. He has really good intentions, always."

"Remember when you told me about three or four weeks ago you were feeling lonely?"

"Yeah… I mean, I've been saying that for most of the time I've been here, but I think I know which time you're talking about."

"You've been saying it a lot less."

"Have I?"

"Is Jace really, really helping that much?"

Dr. Chadwick suddenly turned into a therapist. Her PhD was in cancer studies, but she had two teenage boys of her own. "Boys are dumb, you know that. But I know that boy cares about all one hundred percent of you. If you said you wanted a flower that was growing in a volcano across the world, the only reason he would hesitate to get it would be he would be away from you for too long."

"You're exaggerating."

"Am I? I don't think I am. You know that I have two boys, right?"

Now, as Brooke lie there in the same bed as Jace, with her ear against his chest, she wondered. Would he really do that? Was the stuffed Nemo near his head a real testament to his loyalty? Brooke often compared him to a puppy who grew too fast, and stumbled over his lanky limbs. "Hey, Jace?"

"Yeah? You need some more water or something?" It was a safe assumption, as they hadn't been talking much. Brooke had tears in her eyes and Jace had been awfully stoic. Uncharacteristically stoic.

"If you... Uh..." Brooke struggled for her words. She wasn't even sure why she wanted his attention. "Or, I mean, if I..."

"Are you sleepy? Go to bed, Jesus. You're so stubborn."

"N-no! No, I'm not." She did sound a little congested from crying and she was a little sleepy. Maybe a little bit more than a little bit sleepy. "I just... Never mind. It's dumb."

"Whenever you say something's dumb, I'm at least ninety percent sure it isn't as dumb as you think it is. Or dumb at all, for that matter."

"Okay, maybe it's not dumb. But I still don't want to say it."

"Fine, but you were lying about being sleepy."

"Was not."

"Was too."

The blonde rolled her eyes and took his iPod. She put the right earbud in his hand, and the left earbud in her ear. The cord was a little stretched, but Jace didn't mind. Brooke flipped through his music collection for something to fall asleep to, even though she didn't recognize a lot of his music.

"I could pick something," Jace murmured, gently taking the iPod from her, "if you want. Just relax."

Brooke took the plush Nemo in her hands and hugged it to her chest and waited. A nice piano melody came on, and Jace relaxed as well.

And Jace Aiko Anderson sang her to sleep. He sang and sang and sang as quietly as he could into her tiny ear. She had weirdly tiny ears. Weird. Jace loved singing but was usually embarrassed by it; he felt like people thought he was showing off or something. His mom always told him not to, but that was probably because she hated Bing Crosby for some ungodly reason.

The rain kept a nice beat with the song lyrics and eventually, the melody of the song, her heartbeat, and the rain lined up with each other.

Go ahead
I think you'll be just fine again
Go ahead
I think you'll find your way again

And when you're back I won't be who you're looking for
I've changed, I admit now, but I still have my fun

Chapter Twenty One

May 31st, 2014
9:05am

Oh my god. Oh my god. Oh my god. Where is she? Where's anyone? Holy shit. She didn't tell me she had treatment today. Oh god. Is she dead? No way. I left for three minutes to get flowers and if she wasn't okay I would know. Where is she?

Jace couldn't help but panic.

Maybe she's just not feeling good. Maybe she has an appointment. No. No no no no. I never should have left her alone. This is all my fault. This truly is all of my fault, I'm not even exaggerating. It was all because of that stupid wish.

He began to open random doors when he couldn't find Brooke Kella Boe, or Peter, or May. It was a little intrusive and a little awkward when he would open the door on an exam going on or a couple fighting or something, but it was just a testament to how Jace wasn't good at thinking things through.

The fourth door he opened had Brooke within its walls. It was a recreation room. It didn't have many people in it, and didn't seem to have many lights either. The main light source was a projector in the middle of the room, that looked like it had been run over by a golf cart. Jace wondered how it was working, but he was distracted by what was being projected.

Finding Nemo.

"I shall call him Squishy and he shall be mine and he shall be my Squishy. Come on. Squishy. Come on, little Squishy."

Oh god. I grew up with the goal of becoming Prince Phillip or Eric or something but I ended up as Dory. I just say fluffy and not squishy.

Under the projector was a blanket fort made of sheets and chairs. Jace could see the silhouette of Brooke as well as the form of the stuffed Nemo next to her. His heart rate dropped dramatically from 'holy shit my almost-girlfriend is dead holy crap this is all my fault' to 'aww, she made a blanket fort and she found popcorn and she looks really comfortable and happy.'

She heard him come in, and paused the movie to look back at him. "Oh, hey. I probably should've told you where I was, huh?"

"No, don't worry about it. I would've found you eventually." *Even if you were dead, I would've got to you eventually. Probably wouldn't have taken nearly as long, either.* Jace crossed the room with his long legs covered by the same dark jeans he wore every day. Brooke didn't notice that Jace wore the same thing every day, but Jace reminded Peter of a cartoon character, like Jimmy Turner or Timmy Neutron.

Jace exhaled and took a seat on a little pillow

next to Brooke's throne. "How did you set all of this up while I was gone?" He asked, handing her the bouquet of lilac flowers and holding his own cup of hot chocolate from the lobby. "This is practically a palace."

"Practically? No, it is a palace. My dad set it up for me, and said you might like it too. I think that means something happened with Mom... He only does stuff like this, really radical stuff, when Mom goes off on trips for three weeks or something." Her voice took on a melancholy tone all of a sudden, and her eyes averted from the screen and down toward the white speckled tile and throw blankets. Brooke shook herself as if she was waking up but she just didn't want to think about her mother. "What's the weather like out there?"

"Oh, just June gloom. What's the weather like in here?"

"That's a weird question."

"I know," Jace sipped from his hot chocolate, "I just didn't know what to say."

"You're ridiculous."

"Yep, that's my name. Thanks for letting me know."

A good majority of their conversations and sets of dialogues ended with Brooke rolling her eyes in a playful manner. She leaned her little blonde head on his shoulder and turned her attention back to the movie. Without hesitation, Jace pulled his arm around her figure and remembered that time they played tag in the garden. This was followed by a large, dumb smile. Dumb smiles were so common in both of their emotions now that they were around each other.

"Where'd your dad find the movie?"

"eBay hunting… He was gonna save it for my birthday, but-"

"But there's no better time to watch *Finding Nemo* than on a rainy day, right." Jace didn't like entertaining the thought of Brooke's death while she was around, and he didn't want her thinking about it either. "When's your birthday?"

"October 3rd. I was a 'preemie,' my due date was Halloween."

"Aw, man! That would've been so cool. Now that I think about it, I can remember celebrating your birthday in class. Or, rather, the whole class singing to you while you awkwardly wondered what radical excuse you could come up with to get out of precalc class."

"Yeah…" Brooke picked at the thorns on the roses. "When's your birthday?"

"Guess."

"Halloween? Christmas? Veteran's Day?"

"January fourth, 1997, Clara Barton Hospital." Jace was born in this hospital, and would probably die here. "That's why you never heard about it, we were always on winter break."

"You invited me to your birthday once, though. Like, in third grade. It was one of those things where you just invited the whole class to be nice."

"Yup. Star Wars themed. Best year ever…" Jace began to lightly stroke her arm with his thumb. The movie was coming to a close. "Do you not like celebrating your birthday?"

"Well… I don't feel like there's any point. I won't have that many more of them."

He said nothing and just paused the movie. *Should I tell her now? No. That would be dumb.* "I… I promise, swear to every god ever thought to be in existence, that you'll have plenty more birthdays. And I also promise that I'll be there for everyone, if you want me to. With a stuffed animal and some flowers and a blanket fort building kit."

The petite little girl with the small ears and boney fingers let out a big sigh. It was so big, Jace wondered if it would ever end. Brooke was trying to figure out what to say. "Jace."

"Brooke."

"Jace... I don't want you around when I die."

"You mean, in like a hundred years? Maybe two hundred years. You never know with modern medicine. Remember that movie *Elysium* where they had those big coffin things that you could get into where they would solve your diseases? Wait, not solve, I mean cure. You can't solve diseases." His pace increased quickly. "Unless you could solve diseases. I'm sure there's a lot of math that goes into diseases, right? Is cholera just a giant math problem? Holy shit! Where's that nurse, I have to tell them my theory. I'll win a Nobel Prize. What even is a Nobel Prize? I don't think I want one. Isn't it named after the guy who made dynamite or something?"

Brooke couldn't even take any more of it. She tried to think of the easiest solution to shut him up, and doing something to surprise him was what she concluded was best. Her torso, her face, her lips, moved closer to his own. Panic rushed through her veins. *How the hell do you kiss someone? Okay, just aim. Aim. You got this.*

Chapter Twenty Two

August 13th, 2012
1:43pm

Jace Aiko Anderson was half-Japanese. Plus some other stuff, because Dianne was some weird Russian-Mexican mix, but Aiko Ken was mostly Japanese. There was probably something else weird in there to give him green eyes. He was what someone would call mixed race and what other people would call a mutt.

"There's no way you're Japanese. With that floppy hair?"

"You're just lying to sound cool."

"I asked what race you were, I didn't ask for your entire family tree, Jesus."

"So does that mean you know how to speak Russian and Mexican and Japanese and English? How do you say 'butt' in Russian? And 'I wanna fuck you in the' in Japanese? Chicks eat that shit up, man."

Plus, everyone expecting him to be great at math because he looked partially Asian.

He could remember one day in particular, in his pre-calculus class with Brooke, when someone asked him what his grade point average was. Jace really, really didn't want to say; his mom had already gotten mad at him the night before.

"I've got, uh, a solid 3.5." This was when Brooke figured out just how bad of a liar he was, and it was also when she figured out that he was at least a little sensitive. "Why, what about you?"

The person asking was Travis. Travis would later be known to have thrown Brooke in the pool during the end of the year pool party. But right now, he was just this one asshole who sat behind them in class. "Don't lie. What do you really have?" Travis was the very definition of ignorant, arrogant, pompous and if you looked up ass in a dictionary, you would probably find his face poorly photoshopped onto a donkey. "I've heard you're either the smartest Mexican or the stupidest Japanese."

"Either way, he's smarter than you."

Brooke didn't look up from her math work. She was on problem thirty five and didn't plan on quitting anytime soon, but Travis' very existence might just change her mind.

A big, dumb grin came across his face in the light of her comeback. "You heard her."

"Wow, the mutt and the cute cancer patient. Is this the next John Green book?"

"Jesus, you can't shut up for three seconds, can you? I'm trying to finish my homework, so stop being an asshole."

Jace could still remember what day that was. It was August thirty first and one of the first moments he looked at Brooke like she was the stars and moon. It wasn't a graceful look; in fact, he looked like an idiot. He wasn't even looking at her, he was looking at the ground beneath her feet and was stuck there in a trance like state while he thought.

What finally woke him up was the obnoxious school bell that rang to signal the end of the day. Travis left the classroom in a hurry, as did the rest of the class, seeing it was a Friday. Brooke wouldn't leave until she finished this one problem on her review sheet and Jace wouldn't leave until he could talk to Brooke.

"Thanks, Brooke."

"No problem." She still didn't look up. "He's an asshole anyway."

"No, it means a lot," Jace murmured, fiddling with his backpack strap. Shit, I said I would remember her full name on the first day of class. What was it? "Brooke... Kella Bowen, right?"

"Ooh, so close." She packed her stuff away into her bag.

Jace's frown resembled one of a small boy who just lost a video game for the fifth time. He just wasn't good at flirting, or remembering stuff, or almost anything when he was trying to be good at it. If he couldn't care less about how he shuffled some cards, he would create the perfect shuffle and bridge. "What'd I mess up? I know it wasn't the middle name." *I swear to God, I studied the middle name.*

"Boe, not Bowen."

"Brooke Kella Boe. I'll remember that, I swear to god."

"Right, right."

Chapter Twenty Three

May 31st, 2014
1:59pm

Her lips ended up on his upper lip. They were in the awkward spot between Jace's nose and lips. Brooke chastised herself for being so close and then messing it up. *Should I try to correct it? People in movies and TV shows always make kissing look so easy, damn it.* She went with the panic option instead and jolted away from him.

Jace didn't say anything to her. He had this weird look on his face, with his nose wrinkled up. First, he blinked a couple of times, then he spoke. "Shit, that was weird." His lack of a filter was showing again. He shook his head like he was shaking himself awake. "Wait, what?" *Did I just imagine that? Probably. I do that a lot, after all.*

Brooke was silent when she was nervous, contrary to Jace's nervous banter. Jace also paced and twitched but Brooke sat so still that Jace leaned forward to poke her to make sure she was okay. "You alright there, Brooke?"

She sat there in entire disbelief. "I can't believe I just did that. You're rubbing off on me, I swear." Brooke laughed in an incredibly awkward fashion.

"Wait, you can't believe you did what?"

"What? Nothing, never mind."

"Wait a second. You kissed me, huh?"

"No."

"You did. You kissed me first. You wanted to shut me up so you kissed me. I can't believe Brooke Kella Boe would commit such a cliché act. Somebody write this on the calendar! This will go down in history books. Our grandchildren's children will hear about this day."

"Shut up! You're so annoying."

"I may be annoying but you kissed me so it doesn't matter. I don't care."

"I can take it back, you know."

"Now you're just being stubborn."

His infectious, ear to ear grin had spread to her lips. She just thought he was so stupid. Stupid, for lack of a better word. Incomparable, maybe. Brooke didn't know how to describe him or the way she made him feel. Ridiculous? She finally grumbled, in defeat, "Just forget it, Jace."

Jace shook his head and his grin widened to show his perfect teeth. Four years of braces and he still wore his retainer at night. "Not until you admit it, or take it back or whatever you said."

"You want me to take it back?"

"Try it."

Brooke leaned in to press her lips to his, just as he got a little ahead of himself and moved in closer to her. They practically crashed into each other, but at least Brooke didn't miss this time.

It was a nice little kiss. Brooke never kissed Aaron and Jace had never kissed Courtney, so Brooke's first kiss was with a clumsy, lanky young man who was really bad at math and had a cut on his lip from that one time he tried to carry roses up the stars with his teeth and didn't know how to do almost anything right.

Jace was having a much different first kiss. His was with the most heavenly, the most wonderful, the most mostest in the whole wide world. What did mostest even mean? He didn't know. But he knew it meant something big. This first kiss was with the prettiest, smartest, and most stubborn introverted cancer fighter on the face of the earth, and Jace couldn't have asked for anything more.

Well, if he could redo it all, he would ask for a little more time.

The couple heard footsteps into the room, and both assumed it was Peter. Sure, they were both correct, but their responses weren't.

"Hey guys, I got some cookies from downstairs of you want any."

This prompted a recoil from both Brooke and Jace. Brooke just hit blanket, and didn't fall that far back. Jace, being Jace, overdid the whole 'trying to pretend they weren't just kissing thing' by falling flat on his back and taking down the entire blanket fort with him; chairs and all. The metal chairs came cascading down and while they were both thankful for the cushions of the pillows, Jace probably sustained a few bruises from it.

Peter was also successfully panicked. He said her name in a worried fashion and crossed the room as quickly as he could. Brooke just had a chair that fell on her leg, nothing major, and she was tangled up in a Winnie the Pooh throw blanket. Peter helped get her untangled, got her on her feet, and gave her a chocolate chip cookie from the cafeteria downstairs while Jace writhed in a really uncomfortable knitted blanket, with three chairs joining him.

Wow. I kissed this boy and that's how he reacted. What an idiot. Stupid was the right word to use. Definitely. Ridiculously stupid.

"You guys alright in here?" Peter Boe couldn't tell if Jace Anderson wanted any help in his predicament, so he just looked his daughter over once to make sure she was alright.

Jace's floppy black hair popped out from the rubble of their fort. His face was a bright red and Brooke didn't know if it was because she just kissed him for the first time or if it was because he was drowning in blankets a couple seconds earlier. "Yep!" responded Jace, "all good. We are all good. Yep. Completely fine. I just-" He pushed himself up and then fell to the floor. "We're all good. I swear. Just a couple of bruises. I'm just gonna go... Ouch... Just gonna go get a Band-Aid or something." Awkwardly, Jace shuffled out and slightly tripped right outside the door frame.

It was quiet after Jace left. The only noises were the sound of the end credits for *Finding Nemo* and the soft whirr of the projector. Peter picked up the lavender roses from the speckled floor, then handed them over to his tiny daughter. "Did I tell you... Or did I tell you?"

"Did you tell me what?"

"Jason whatever whatever is head over heels for you and you know it."

"Dad?"

"Yeah?"

"He's been here for three weeks. Stop pretending you don't know his name."

Chapter Twenty Four

September 18th, 2002
8:12am

It was her first day of kindergarten. His first day of first grade and her first day of kindergarten was the first day Jace Aiko Anderson saw Brooke Kella Boe. And he could remember it better than any other memory in the whole world. It was a real testament to how he felt about her, because he could never remember anything.

It was a cold September day and Jace could remember it being really windy, like ridiculously and annoyingly windy. Perhaps this was the reason why Jace could remember the tiny little girl so well, because her twin braids of light hair swirled around prominently in the wind.

Twin braids and bright eyes and a purple dress and a white backpack and a shit ton of goosebumps because it was really cold that day, even for Jace, who wore a big jacket. He wore that jacket nearly every day until he was in sixth grade, then wore a hoodie until high school, then realized he didn't have to hide underneath a jacket all the time. He didn't need armor once he was comfortable with himself.

Another thing Jace remembered oh so well about the tiny girl was that she wasn't so tiny. Now, in the year 2014, she was only 5'2" and barely skin and bone. But back then, she was a big kid. Or Jace remembered her being big. Maybe she was just intimidating.

And this may not come as a surprise to anyone, but Jace never worked up the nerve to talk to Brooke until they were in that one pre-calculus class with Mr. Rivera - the man who was believed not to have any arms because he always wore this one sweatshirt even when it was really hot outside. So, naturally, every high schooler assumed he had no arms. Right. Casimir Pulaski High School.

Point is, Jace knew Brooke for a very short time before he was gone.

Chapter Twenty Five

June 1st, 2014
8:57am

Today was the day.

Today would be the day that Jace Aiko Anderson would open up his chest and pour out everything he had been keeping from Brooke. After weeks of the nice kisses and the 'not so awkward anymore' silences and the hundreds of dollars in roses, Jace finally figured it was time to tell her the truth. He didn't have a lot of time left, anyway.

Brooke was also thinking about today being a special day. Today, she felt, would be the day she died.

Nothing hurt, but nothing felt right either. The hospital was in a dreary, slowed down dream like state; like the calm before the storm. Her calcium levels had been all over the place lately, despite her treatments, and the chemo was only helping a little bit. But it also could've been all in her head.

Today, Brooke prayed to anyone who would listen that Jace wouldn't come to visit her today. *Just... Let him have work today, or something. I couldn't handle knowing he was here.* Having her parents, her father there was enough trauma for her. They sat against the wall, sleeping.

Today, Jace prayed to anyone who would listen

that Brooke would just believe him, or that she wouldn't be mad. He didn't understand why she would be mad, but he never understood people's emotions in the first place.

Brooke, there's something I have to tell you. Brooke, can I talk to you alone for a second? Hey, Brooke, I've got this really life shattering thing to tell you but I'm really bad at words so I might just show you but that might freak you out and why the hell did I think I could do this? I screwed all of this up for her and now I just came down to try and fix it and I won't even know if it works. Damn damn damn damn damn. I gotta get out of here. No. Just keep swimming.

Jace did not climb up the stairs two at a time. He didn't get coffee for Peter, he didn't jump with joy. Today... Today was different.

Fourth floor.

Room thirty three.

Four.

Three.

Three.

Four hundred and thirty three.

Today was different. The clouds screamed it as him while he walked by every window. The cracks on the stairs and the chipped paint on the railing bid him farewell, and the squeaky door between floors two and three cried out for him. Damn, I'm attached to a building. A stairwell. It's a like a Greek tragedy up in here.

Today is different.

With each step, his foot felt heavier and heavier. It was like someone added a chain link with every move he made. Everything hurt, but the pain of dreading seeing her was nothing compared to actually seeing her.

Her.

Brooke Kella Boe.

Literally the very reason he was on this earth at this moment, holding these flowers with these trembling, rough fingers. Her.

"H-hey..." he managed to choke. "How're you feeling, Nemo?" Jace told himself to stop having a breakdown when she was the actual sick one, but it was way harder than it sounded. He crossed the room and kissed her forehead, then her nose, then her lips. "Listen, I've gotta talk to you, Brooke. Do you think we could go out to the garden?"

"But I'm so sleepy..." She groaned and pulled the pillow over her eyes. Sleepiness wasn't a good sign either. Usually Brooke was bouncing out of bed to start some dumb adventure with Jace, to listen to his golden voice and feel his healing touch. Now, she was just scared. "Is everything okay?"

"Uh... Um," Jace chuckled, forcing a smile, "sorta. It will be. C'mon, I'll carry you. You ready?" His voice cracked and faded in and out like a broken radio.

A short nod prompted him to take the tiny girl into his arms and down the elevator. His heart felt like it had stopped again. Everything screamed at him to not do it. Everything from the grass to his bones to his eyelashes to his chapped lips that feared for a Brooke-less future.

Jace studied her. Her eyes were still the brightest thing for miles. He always admired her bright eyes as he had dull grey ones that he had inherited from his mother. She had three little freckles in the shape of a triangle on her right arm. Under her chin, she had a scar from when she was playing at a woodchip play ground. Finally, peeking out from behind her hospital gown was the scar from her scapula removal. Her bad wing. Her beautiful, special tiny fin. *What did Marlin call it in the movie? I just watched this the other day, now it's gonna bother me... Lucky!*

Her lucky fin.

Not many people were up this early, so at least they had their privacy in the gardens. Desolate as it had been those weeks ago, the rain was bringing some flowers back up. There were now tiny, purple flowers in the field they had run in and a little bit of Jace's nose imprint was still there. It made his solemn face light up with a sort of melancholy joy. *I made her happy and I helped her get healthy. And that's all that matters. Right?*

Just keep swimming. Just keep swimming. Just keep swimming. Just keep swimming. Just. Keep. Swimming. He was Dory and that meant he could make it through anything.

Jace took a seat at the bench and sat with Brooke in his lap. "Hey... You awake?"

"Mmhmm, I'm up... Kinda. What's goin' on?" Brooke could only slightly tell that something was wrong. She kinda just wrote it off as her tired and slightly angry state of mind. "Did you wanna start another mud fight? Because I don't know if I'm up for that right now. Give me a little bit to wake up."

"Wait, what's wrong with you?"

"What?" Brooke mumbled, blinking awake.

"Why are you sad?" Jace eyed her suspiciously. "You're sad. I can tell. Something's wrong." He began to look her over, from head to toe.

Brooke turned her head and blindly lied. "I just don't feel good."

"What does not good mean? Not good isn't good.

I mean, that's the definition but if you say you're not good then you're really not good because you're one of the toughest people I know."

Brooke half-hissed, half-groaned, "You know what I mean. I'm done. I'm finished. It's over. And I don't want you to be here for it. I thought... Maybe I could just sleep through it."

Damn. Keep it together, Jace. "No. Stop. Just... Hear me out." *Just. Keep. Swimming.*

"There's no way you could possibly know that I'm not going to die. I've gotten past the point of denial, and it's time you did too. I'm really, really sorry, Jace. I... I tried to warn you. I'm so sorry."

Jace sat there quietly, lips pressed together. *Crap. No. Don't say it. Don't explode.*

And guess what he did?

He exploded.

"You're not going to die. I swear on everything, I swear on my life and the fate of the whole universe and mankind that you are not going to die of this cancer. You're going to die old and happy somewhere, while you're sleeping and surrounded by people who love you. You are not going to die in this God forsaken hospital, alright?"

"There's no way you could possibly know that."

"But I do."

"Stop! You don't! You don't and you never will. Just leave me alone, alright?" He didn't understand and would never understand how much it hurt for him to offer her hope, on a silver platter, just to have someone else steal it away. Someone else, some imaginary being of fate.

Jace knew she didn't mean it. Or, at least, hoped to God she didn't mean it. This whole quest couldn't have been for nothing. Even if she didn't mean it, her words crushed his no longer beating heart. "I'll leave you alone if you hear me out."

Brooke's silence was taken by Jace as an agreement. But now, she wouldn't even look at him. Her eyes were cast down, staring at a weed growing between two slabs of concrete.

"Okay…" He began to stutter, and his hands danced around each other. "You're probably cold, huh? Here, take my jacket. I don't want you getting another cold, that was awful last time. I thought your mom was going to kill me-"

"Are you just going to tell me about how you slept in the stairwell for the first few days you were visiting? Because I know about that. My dad isn't good at keeping secrets."

"I didn't even know that your dad knew that!

How does he know that?"

"Why'd you sleep on the stairs? Why didn't you just go home?" Brooke's tone of voice was rising in her confusion, manifesting itself as anger. She wanted to know. She wanted to know why he couldn't go home and why he was so damn confusing when he was supposed to be the only one in the world she could truly trust. "Tell me the truth. Then go home. I'm sure your mom misses you."

"I'm t-trying, I'm trying really hard. It's… W-way harder than you think. It's way harder than I-I thought it would be. It's complicated. I've been rehearsing this for months and I still can't do it. Oh god. Okay. I can do this, I swear. I just… I'm dead."

Chapter Twenty Six

June 6th, 2013
11:14am

"Mr. and Mrs. Boe, your daughter has another tumor. It's a grade four tumor, because it's what she had before, which is Ewing Sarcoma. Hopefully chemo will help, but we cannot operate until we know more. I'm sorry."

Brooke knew on that day that nothing was good if Dr. Chadwick wasn't there. She was like Brooke's coin of good luck or a stuffed animal she held onto; it was so ineffably comforting to have her there.

This doctor, a young and somewhat inexperienced-looking man, politely excused himself from the room.

A routine checkup was all this started out as. She just had some weird bruise on her rib cage that she assumed she got in her sleep or something. Nothing real to be concerned about. Now, they were here.

Her ill-hearted wish had come true. After her huge argument with her mother, Brooke Kella Boe went to bed with the thought that she wouldn't have to deal with May if she had cancer. She wouldn't have to deal with school and Aaron and Travis and her mother's consistent disappointment. *If I had cancer again, then she'd be sorry.*

And damn, she was right.

May broke out in a fit of tears. Peter's reaction was even scarier because he didn't do anything. He couldn't do anything, not until Brooke said something, so he just looked expectantly at her. "Brooke, you alright, hun?"

"Huh? Yeah… I'm fine."

"Are you sure?"

"Yeah. I mean…" Brooke ran her hands over her face and through her hair. At least Aaron was already gone, so she wouldn't have to tell him. "I guess…" She couldn't find the words and Peter didn't blame her.

May tried her best to contain herself, to keep herself from becoming a blubbering wreck like she did when her little girl got diagnosed with Ewing Cancer all those years ago. She didn't want to go through that again.

"I think…" A sheepish, happy smile started to form on Brooke's face. "'Every time it rains, it stops raining. Every time you hurt, you heal. After darkness, there is always light and you get reminded of this every morning but still you choose to believe that the night will last forever. Nothing lasts forever…' Remember that quote, dad? You bought me that poster and hung it up in my room for my fifteenth birthday."

"Nothing lasts forever, not the good, or the bad."

"So you might as well smile while you're here, right?"

Peter could not put into words how much he admired his daughter. He would spend the majority of his life trying to. She wasn't given much, she had to work for a lot of what she had. Brooke wasn't born into the gifted elementary track or anything. Yes, she was smart, but it was always because she desperately wanted to be smart. Brooke wanted to be like her mother, and help people. Even if that changed, her level of intelligence didn't.

His irises were swimming in pools of clear tears. Happy, bittersweet tears. "You really are the best daughter anyone could ever hope for, you know that? That cancer bullshit - I mean, stuff," Peter corrected himself in front of May, "won't stand a chance against my little Nemo."

And that, even though Brooke just found out she had a dangerous malignant tumor in her ribs, that moment was one of the best she ever had to that point. Peter practically represented everything that was good with the world. And May shattered the moment just as fast as she could.

"Do you understand how expensive this is, Brooke?" May Sanderson Boe stopped shaking. "This isn't anything to laugh at, either of you. This is serious."

"I know, Mom, but I can make it through it. Don't you think I can?"

"You can, but it means I'll be working every day

of the week for fourteen hours. You're not the only one fighting here, Brooke. You're so selfish."

Brooke began to shout without any warning signs of her bubbling anger. "I'm so selfish? I'm the selfish one?" After hopping off the examination table, she began to gather her clothes. "I can't even believe you. With your damn campaganeh."

"You watch your mouth, young lady!"

"I will if you watch yours. I'll stop cussing the day you stop drinking." And with that, Brooke pushed the door open and headed towards the nice woman at the front desk, to find out her room was on the fourth floor so she could sit alone.

Alone was what she wanted. Lonely was what she got.

May hissed, "It's pronounced *champagne*! Don't you walk away from me."

"I guess we know where she gets her temper from... And her intelligence. And her stubbornness. She gets her vocabulary from me, though, so I get some credit." Peter was really, really just trying to lighten the mood. He didn't want the only two people and the most important people in his life to be fighting. He really didn't have anyone else; Peter wasn't the most social.

"You're just as much to blame for this."

"You're right."

"You- Wait, you think I'm right?"

"You are. I'm just as much to blame for Brooke's cancer as she is. Because she isn't responsible for it and neither am I."

Chapter Twenty Seven

June 1st, 2014
9:18am

"You're… Dead."

"I'm dead."

She just stared at him. "You mean metaphorically or what?"

"N-no. I physically… I'm here to help you and that's it. You l-literally are my sole purpose for living or existing or w-whatever the term is. That's how I know you're not going to die."

Her silence signaled him to keep going, even if it was somewhat hesitantly.

"I… Um… I've been healing you. That's why you thought it was the kick before you died. It's really, really hard to explain, but I'm gonna try… I'm here - down here, I mean - because I wanted to be there for you and help you even though you probably wouldn't even need help, because you'd kick this cancer in the balls… But anyway… Jesus, this is really hard. I don't know how to explain it without sounding like an idiot. Not that I'm not already an idiot. I know I'm an idiot.."

Brooke's silence stunned him into his own terrified silence. He couldn't even look at her eyes anymore, as they turned red. Her fists curled up, and she whispered, "Do you think this is funny?"

Silence. But this one was a little more confused. "Wait, what?"

"Do you really," her voice began to crack and she quickly corrected it, "really think that it's okay to come here and do that?"

"Wait, I don't- what?" What was even happening? Where did any of this come from? Girls don't make any sense. People don't make any sense, but girls especially don't.

"You think it's funny to come to my hospital room and kiss my lips and sleep in my bed and make me fall incredibly, stupidly in love with you?"

"But I didn't- Wait. You're in love with me?"

"And then you just play this awful, awful joke. Why? Because someone told you I'm agnostic? Is that what you're getting at here, did you come just to preach the word of God? Or do you just get a kick out of being mean to people? Because I have some news for you."

Every word was a dagger in Jace's chest. The pain was similar to having one's fingernails pulled off, to being punched in the face repeatedly, to being shot over and over again with different types of guns. It was worse than being run over by a giant Ford truck when he was inside a tiny old Toyota Camry. And he would know.

It hurt so much because she didn't believe him. "P-please, let me explain…"

"No. No, I've heard enough. If you are some terrible, twisted sort of priest, and you believe in the heaven and hell and the whatever, that's fine. I don't care. But you're going to your damn hell if you think it's alright to make people fall in love with you and then turn around and lie to them. What the hell is wrong with you?"

Her tiny, pale face turned the color of the tips of the roses Jace brought to her every day: a bright red. Jace never associated the color with anger before this point, the color red was the color of her blush up to this point.

Then, she began to sneeze. It was a lot harder to take her seriously with her little sneezes. The cutest sneezes in the world. "Brooke, you didn't even listen to me. I know it sounds impossible or dumb or cliché but you have to listen to me before you write me off as some Westboro Baptist Church member."

"You know, I wish I knew what that was, I know it's something bad but I don't have to listen to you."

She tried to get away from him and run, but she just rolled out of his lap and ended up on the sidewalk. Then she ripped the jacket from her shoulders. "I'm not going to listen to you. I've already accepted that I'm going to die. You don't have to sugarcoat it with this stupid angel bullshit." Brooke, despite her best efforts to not injure herself, landed on her hands and knees. All four points of contact began to bleed.

"Look, Brooke… Nemo, listen."

Brooke stopped holding her anger back. Her hand flew at a million miles an hour to make contact with his cheek.

"Don't you dare call me that again."

Chapter Twenty Eight

January 1st, 2014
10:00am

Dianne West's wedding date was set for January first. It was her fiancé, Sam's idea. "A new beginning," he told her, "it's symbolic and everything." He was a writer, so Jace wasn't surprised to hear a dumb and cheesy idea like that from him.

She would be three months pregnant on their wedding. And she wished she would've known that before she bought her wedding dress and had to get it slightly tailored.

Sam was paying for most of the wedding. Dianne's parents weren't alive anymore and she barely had enough money to feed herself, her son and their dog, so Jace was working three jobs; he was a waiter, worked at the pet store, and at a cheap tourist gift shop with those dumb little knickknacks for people from out of country. He hated most of the hours he spent working. It was all out of the love for his mother. Sam was alright, he could've been far worse as far as Jace was concerned. His mother didn't expect Jace to call Sam 'Dad' or anything, so that was pretty good.

"The colors are deep green and light blue. All of the men will have blue button-up shirts and green coats. And black bow ties, because who doesn't love black bow ties?"

With a dramatic head roll from both of them, Sam and Jace groaned.

Dianne would jokingly snap, "Hey, what did I tell you two?"

They moaned again in unison. "We picked the colors and you get to pick everything else."

Jace's mother would then smile, kiss her son on the cheek and then her soon-to-be husband on the lips, and go off to plan something else. Dianne put so much sweat and so many tears into this wedding. If she could have, she would've done anything to make sure it wasn't snowing on January first. The wedding was indoors, but she hated the snow.

The odds weren't in her favor. But were they ever?

On the night of December thirty first, a layer of snow covered the grass and a layer of frost covered the roads. And Jace was the unlucky soul who had to drive Dianne and Sam Sierze to their wedding.

Maybe, Dianne would later reflect, the events of that day wouldn't have happened if Sam didn't see her in her wedding dress. They always said it was bad luck, and from that day on, Dianne West Sierze lived her years out with a momentous superstition filled routine. This routine would be one of the causes of Sam's divorce claim with her in the coming months.

Jace drove his mother's outdated, rusty Toyota Camry with the couple in the back. The lovely, happy couple that Jace couldn't have been more excited for. He just wanted his mother to be happy and healthy and not thousands of dollars in debt. Sometimes he was the one taking care of her, instead of the other way around.

The dining hall where the wedding was to be held was only half an hour away. Jace prepared his radio stations and his map so he wouldn't have to pay any attention to whatever the soon to be newly weds were talking about. He always felt bad about eavesdropping.

January first was off to a great start when Mom was five minutes late and her hair wasn't all curled. Then, they hit about every red light on the way to the dining hall.

The frosting on the three-level wedding cake was the fire engine red semi truck that plowed into their happy little life. And the silence after the crash, with the snow falling down, was the reason he was so deathly afraid of silences. The silence where he sat, half conscious, feeling like he was bleeding from every pore in his body. The last thing that Jace remembered seeing was the cloudy sky, and the cloud shaped like a broken heart. His mind went blank.

"Where is he? Where's my boy?" Like a mother bear or lion, Dianne charged through Clara Barton Hospital. It looked like something out of a horror movie; her makeup was smeared by tears and snow, and blood was splattered all over her wedding dress. A cut on her cheek was sewn up with stitches and Sam's tuxedo jacket was around her shoulders. She screamed at the young girl at the desk, "Tell me where my boy is!"

This young girl ripped her earbuds out at the sight. She was trained for situations like this, though. "Ma'am, please calm down. I'm sure your son is being taken care of. What is his name?"

"Jace. Jace Aiko Anderson." Tears and short breaths interrupted her nervous rant. "I named him after his father. He's a beautiful boy, he's tall and has his dad's floppy hair and a little scar on his cheek where he fell off his bike when he was little…" Sam took his fiancée's shoulder in an attempt to comfort her, but she pulled away.

"Room, uh…" The panic was getting to the woman behind the desk as well. "You'll have to wait in the waiting room on the third floor. A doctor will be out to update you soon."

Third floor. She tried to burst into the stairwell but the door wouldn't open at first, so she slammed into the metal. Sam pushed the door open for her. He really didn't know what to do. He had been sheltered his whole life and never lost anyone like this. Initially, he thought the stitches he needed on his arm were a big deal. But Jace broke four bones and fractured most of his ribs.

Dianne tore her shoes off and ran up the stairs, two at a time. She arrived at the waiting room and could do nothing but sit.

Sam stood outside, making a phone call he knew he shouldn't be making.

Chapter Twenty Nine

June 1st, 2014
9:20am

Her bony, beautiful fingers seared his cheekbone.

"I never want to see you again."

Brooke figured this wasn't that dramatic of a request. He might come back. He might come back to torture her. But now, she could die. The reason she wanted to live, to take care of this clumsy boy, was completely abolished. She always knew she never needed anyone. She knew since she was a little girl she wouldn't get married. There aren't happy endings; her parents were proof of that, his parents were proof of that, and now they would continue the tradition.

But even when she slapped him, she felt his glow.

No. No. Brooke, don't do this. You're making a mistake. I would never do that to you, I just wanted to help. I love you. I need you, so much. You mean so much to me. I probably could've said that better but I swear, it's not as bad as it sounds...

These were the things Jace Aiko Anderson wanted to say with his golden voice to the girl with the lucky fin.

"I... Okay."

This is what he said to her.

And with that, Brooke Kella Boe walked away from the boy who gave her the will to live. *Stay,* something told her. *Stay. Stay. He means so much to you, and you mean so much to him. Stay. Stay.* Maybe it was the part of him that had infiltrated her soul. It was the glow that stuck with her. *No.*

Hours went by. Jace listened to her departing footsteps, the door opening, the door closing, and even tried to hear the pitter patter of her little feet on the floor. By now, he was laying on the ground, in the mud. He stared at the roses she left there. His mind, for only the second time ever, was blank. Mud soaked into his pores and his jacket and his hair. Mud squished between his fingers and between his toes and into his shoes. His jacket was pulled over his face. He hoped, maybe, someone would find him out here and think he was dead. Jace wanted to be dead.

Well, he wanted to be dead again. He wanted to be back up in the clouds, where he could just watch her be happy. He could send her nice things and try to heal her from afar, even if it didn't work as well. But she was happier back then.

"Bring me back."

He furred his brows and said it again. "Bring me back."

He waited for a 'beam me up, Scotty' sort of moment. He was told, if he said those words, he could return home. Maybe he didn't say it loud enough.

Chapter Thirty

January 1st, 2014
10:53am

Jace was moved to room three hundred and one from the emergency room. He was unconscious and couldn't breathe on his own. His body was covered in bruises and cuts and debris. Dianne and Sam followed his barely breathing corpse up the stairs and sat in silence until the door opened again.

The man standing there was one neither of them recognized. Well, not immediately. Dianne West, soon to be Dianne Sierze, squinted. Her nose wrinkled up in the same way Jace's did. "Who are you? Get out."

"Ma'am, I'm... I'm sorry. I was, uh..."

The nurse next to him began to pull the words out of his mouth like there was a ribbon hanging from his lips. "Ms. West, please calm down. This man was driving the truck that crashed into your Camry, Ms. West. He came to speak to you."

The trucker didn't look very out of the ordinary. Murderers usually had this look in their eye, or blood on their clothes or just a suspicious air. This man had none of those things. He was one of the kindest, most sympathetic people Dianne ever saw and would ever see again. "I'm so, so sorry, ma'am. It's entirely my fault." His voice was spiced with a southern accent. "It's just... The snow... I'm not used to snow, ma'am. My name's Earl, Earl Koski, nice to meet you. I just... Wish it was under better circumstances."

Sam spoke on the behalf of his torn wife. "I'm Sam, and this is Dianne."

Earl nodded and looked to the hospital bed. "Is that your boy?"

"Hers. Not mine."

"What's his name?"

"Jace," Dianne spoke up, "Jace Aiko Anderson. He just graduated from high school. His birthday is in three days."

"I..." The southern man struggled for anything to say. He had never been a talker, that's why he took a job where he could just drive for miles on end. It had been so relaxing up until now. "I have twins. They're both in seventh grade right now, bless their hearts. Li'l Sammie and Anna. Theys' birthday was a couple days ago. I didn't get to be there, though. They're growing up into two fine little girls..." Earl quickly corrected himself. "Sorry, miss, this isn't about me. What I'm tryin' to say is... I have kids. And I can only try to imagine how much you're hurtin'. I'm so, so sorry."

And that was when, in despite of Dianne's anger, decided not to press charges against the man in the fire engine red truck. Anyone with kids wouldn't do that intentionally. And her boy had to go without a father; why should his daughters?

"Thank you, sir," Sam stood, "but we need to grieve alone."

"Alright. I'll be outside for a li'l while longer, in case you want to go over anything."

As Earl walked out, someone else walked in. There were a million people that Dianne prayed for; a nurse to say Jace would be alright, or a doctor, or that girl he liked so much. Wasn't she staying in this hospital? Maybe it was some of her own family who heard the news. Anyone was welcome in here.

Except for the one man who entered.

Aiko Ken Anderson.

The beeping of Jace's life support system created a haunting sort of soundtrack.

"Aiko? What are you doing here?" Sam only ever saw pictures of his fiance's ex, and he had turned into he who shall not be named around the house. He tried to sound surprised.

Beep. Beep. Beep.

Beep. Beep. Beep.

Sirens nearby, the forced breathing, the snow falling, her heart beating and her son's heart slowing.

"Get out." Dianne didn't even look at him.

"No! No, Dianne. I called him here."

Quiet.

Quiet.

Quiet.

Dianne looked at her fiance. She just stared at his square jawline, and the freckles on his neck and the stitches on his arm. She just stared, and it scared the absolute shit out of Sam. Her eyes were so intense, unlike her son's. "Why would you do that, Samuel?"

Sam knew he was in deep shit when she referred to him by his full name instead of a nickname or a pet name. "He - I... I thought he would wanna know, Dianne. I called him a couple hours ago."

Aiko still had said nothing.

"Why wouldn't you ask me?"

"Because I knew you wouldn't let me, sweetheart. I'm sorry, but I... I k-know how much Jace cared about him. Just give him a minute, please." Sam never thought he would be here, vowing for his fiancé's ex husband. He hated Aiko. He hated everything Aiko did. But Sam really liked Jace and wanted to respect him. He was, after all, letting him marry his mother.

"Please." Aiko whispered, with that golden voice Dianne fell for. "Let me."

Chapter Thirty One

January 1st, 2014
11:30am

"Yeah, I'm fine. But the kid… The kid isn't… No. I don't… I don't know how I'll live with myself. It should be me layin' there not him. He just graduated, she said. Barely a kid… Yeah, I'm fine. I'm fine, I'm fine, I promise. I'll talk to you later, babe. Alright. Love you too."

Earl flipped his phone shut with his chin. His knee bounced in his nervous, adrenaline filled state as he sat outside of room three hundred and one, wishing he had a beer or a cigarette or his big pitbull to pet. For him, the world was falling apart. He couldn't imagine how that nice lady in the wedding gown was feeling.

Another silhouette made its way towards Earl's humble little bench. *Another visitor for Jason, or whatever his name was. Jesus, did I forget the kid's name already? You're such a sack of shit, Earl.*

This shadow instead took a seat next to Earl. It held two plastic cups. Upon investigation, Mr. Koski realized he had seen this shadow before. It was when he was walking up the stairs. This man had been walking down. He had a kind, apologetic smile and wrinkled hands and a tired face.

"I'm sorry to intrude, but you looked like you needed a little coffee."

Earl was nothing short of stunned. There was a long pause before he spoke to the shadow, "Thanks. Uh, who are you?"

"Peter, Peter Boe. Nice to meet you."

"Earl. Where did you, um, where did you come from?" Was this man some guardian angel or something? He hoped so. His mother told him as a kid that there was always a guardian angel following him, and would only appear if he really needed it. Earl just always imagined it being a pretty girl or something, though, not a middle aged man.

"My daughter practically lives here. She's with her mother right now, getting chemotherapy. She's fighting Ewing Cancer. Er, sarcoma. Ewing Sarcoma."

Earl's problems felt very small all of a sudden. "Oh... I'm sorry, sir."

"She's the strongest little girl in the whole wide world, I swear... But you looked like you needed some coffee."

"I did," he faked a chuckle, "Actually. Thank you."

The two grown men sat side by side, watching nurses walk back and forth. Nurses and doctors and patients and family. Hospitals are such a diverse place. There are people of all shapes and sizes and colors and religions but nobody's fighting. Everyone's praying for everyone else. Why is tragedy the only thing to bring people together?

Peter finally asked what he was dying to ask. "Why are you here?"

"I, uh... Car accident."

"Oh, I'm sorry. Who's in there?" Peter jabbed a thumb back at the wall behind them.

"A kid and his mom. She's fine, and I got out fine. I was in my big ol' truck and I ran over their li'l Toyota..." Earl took a deep and shaky breath, "It should be me in there. Not that kid." He took a sip of the coffee but then just let it warm his hands. The warmth was comforting, reminded him of home, where there wasn't any of this snow bullshit. How did people live with it? "He's only eighteen. He didn't even get a shot at life. I wonder if he got accepted into any of 'em fancy schools. I always wanted to go to school. He might never get to get married, or buy a big fancy house somewhere. It's not fair, you know? I've lived my life. He's barely got a shot at his..." Tears welled up in his eyes. *Keep it together, Earl. Men don't cry. Not in front of other men. The only person who's ever seen you cry is Tom. We're gonna keep it that way. Tom always said it was okay, though.*

He furiously wiped at his eyes. "Sorry, Pete. Just a little upset 'bout these kinda things."

"No, please, keep going if you need to." Peter was no stranger to emotion.

"No, it's fine. I just... It gives ya a real perspective on life, when shit like this happens. That poor kid has friends and family and probably a boyfriend 'er a girlfriend who's bawlin' their eyes out. Maybe a girl like one a' my girls. He probably has a baseball team he coaches full of kids who'll never see him again. Isn't that so messed up? And it's all... Is all because of me."

"Do you know what, Earl? Do you have a wife?"

"No. Just a..." Earl always had to be careful about who he told this to. But now he was up north, and it was supposedly different here. "I've got a partner."

"And you have kids with them?" Peter didn't even bat an eye and it made Earl feel infinitely more comfortable.

"Two li'l girls."

"And you want to know how to make up for this?"

How did he know that? *He is some guardian angel or somethin' like that.* "Yeah, I really want to."

"You go home. You quit your job. You get another job. It might pay less, but as long as you get to be around-"

"Tom, Sammie and Anna."

"As long as you get to be around Tom and Sammie and Anna, it's worth it. You could be sleeping in a cardboard box but if they're your real family, they won't care. You treat everyone like they're your kids or your husband. And then you treat your family like they're five times better than that, alright?"

"Sounds like you're speaking from experience."

"You might say that I'm an expert in screwing things up. But, that also makes me an expert in fixing things." Peter clapped Earl's shoulder, then stood. "I've gotta go see what my daughter's up to. It was nice talking to you, Earl. I hope everything works out."

"Oh, uh, thanks. Thanks so much, Peter."

Earl concluded, as Peter walked off into the proverbial sunset that really was just a hospital hallway, that Peter was a guardian angel.

Chapter Thirty Two

June 1st, 2014
9:23am

Brooke was happy to get away from Jace Aiko Anderson as fast as she could. She didn't want him to see her cry. She didn't want him to think he had won a little game that she didn't know they were playing. He cheated. It wasn't fair.

Nothing was fair. Nothing is fair and nothing would ever be fair.

Her tears were abundant but quiet. She wasn't a loud crier, like her mother, but rather a silent one like her father. Tears streamed down Brooke's red cheeks as she ran up the stairs. She tripped in the middle of her furious scurrying, her knee making contact with the concrete and tearing the skin. Brooke hardly noticed, to be completely honest. Her knees and hands were already bleeding, so what did it matter?

It was cliché to say there was too much pain in her heart for her to notice, but it was true. There could literally be an earthquake and Brooke would just think it was her own mind being ruptured by the fact that the kindest boy she ever knew would do something like that. The kindest, most beautiful boy with the golden voice wronged her.

Finally, she arrived in room four hundred and thirty three to find it empty.

Empty except for the dozens upon dozens of flowers Jace had brought her over the last month. Rage overtook her. She went blind and just let her fingers do whatever they pleased.

Peter came up the stairs with a cup of coffee and a chocolate chip cookie. He wasn't expecting Brooke to be in there. *She's probably with her new boyfriend,* he thought. *Brooke and Jace sitting in a tree, K-I-S-S-I-N-G. Ha, there are no trees.* He was expecting a quiet, floral hospital room where he could sit and think about what really happened at the end of Inception.

What he came across was an entirely different scene.

It wasn't floral. Not anymore.

It was quiet, though. But not the sort of quiet he wanted. It was the quiet before the people came out of their houses to see the damage after a storm, the quiet before riots erupted and the quiet after a war was over. It was calamitous in the absolute worst way possible.

The floor was littered with rose petals. No, it was literally covered. There were a few thorns here and there, but for the most part, the white speckled floor was covered in lavender petals and yellow petals with red tips.

"Purple's your favorite color, right? I'll bring you purple next time," he told her.

"Why'd you pick the yellow ones?"

"I dunno. I just thought they looked pretty, I guess."

It wouldn't be until much later that Brooke would discover the meaning of yellow roses with red-tipped petals was friendship that blossomed into love. She would forever wonder if Jace knew that when he picked them out.

A lot of petals were on the floor, sure, but so many more were out the window. Brooke took the bouquets of roses, opened the fourth story window, and threw them as far as she could. They, as luck would have it, landed in the garden where Jace used to lie.

Her tiny, pale hands were covered in cuts from the thorns. Blood mixed with tears while she held her face in her hands.

The scariest part was seeing her bleeding silently on the floor. It was similar to something out of a horror movie, in Peter's eyes. Blood ran down her hands and landed on the petals. All of it was so... Cinematic, as if someone planned it all.

"Honey? Nemo," he scrambled over to her, "what on earth happened?"

Brooke could do nothing more than shake her head. Everything hurt, internally and externally. In her arms was her rugged Eeyore stuffed animal. Trying to say something, Brooke's lips parted but just continued to shake.

Peter had no clue what was happening or what had happened. But he was good at fixing things. He held his seventeen year old daughter as if she were a five year old who had just seen a terrifying movie or whose dog just died.

May, who was actually at Clara Barton Hospital that day, walked into the room, half-distracted by her phone. She stumbled upon the scene and made eye contact with her husband. Afraid to say anything, May made a couple of wild, confused gestures toward their daughter, to which Peter could only shrug.

Brooke worked up the nerve, the strength to say something. Not even a syllable had escaped her lips before she began choking again.

"Deep breaths, sweetheart. Deep breaths."

She listened to her father's advice. In a few more moments, she was ready to try again. "H-he told me… That he was d-dead. Like, an an- angel. And he," Brooke coughed, "was here to heal me, or s-something. That's r-ridiculous, right?" Now that she was talking it would be hard to stop her. "An awful joke. The only r-reason he came here was to mess with me. W-why would he do that?"

"Why would he do that?" echoed Peter. Peter got

to know Jace pretty well, as they bonded over sitting in the hospital room together while Brooke had chemotherapy treatment, and he didn't seem like the type for cruel practical jokes. He could barely tell a joke, let alone plan one. "C'mon, sweetheart, let Mom clean you up. I'll go talk to the nurses about cleaning up in here, okay?"

May took her daughter with open, extended arms and a confused look on her face. Peter was left alone.

Not lonely. Alone, but with a cause. A new sense of purpose.

His feet carried him outside of room four hundred and thirty three. They carried him down the hallway, to the elevator. He slammed his finger on the button with the faded braille lettering that read 'ground floor.'

Sure, he lied about where he was going. Yes, May and Brooke would come back to room four three three and it would still be covered in rose petals. But he was sure that what he was doing was right.

There was a stop at every floor. *Of course,* Peter Boe thought, *with my luck.*

His feet then continued their journey. They took him past the front desk, past the waiting room, and out the front door. He chanted to himself.

"Oh shut up. Every time it rains, it stops raining. Every time you hurt, you heal. After darkness, there is always light and you get reminded of this every morning but still you choose to believe that the night will last forever. Nothing lasts forever. Not the good or the bad. So you might as well smile while you're here."

Chapter Thirty Three

January 1st, 2014
11:57am

And there they stood.

Dianne West versus Aiko Anderson, round two. Referee: Sam Sierze.

Aiko would never hit Dianne. He had a hard time hitting anyone. This fight was all in the mind. It was a battle of looks, a battle of intimidation, a battle of guilt. And it felt like it lasted for years.

"You disappear for eight years of Jace's life, and you come now."

"Yeah. I did."

"And you expect me to treat you like I would've back then? Like you mean something to him, or you mean something to me?"

"I..."

"And you want me to let you back in? For him? You weren't there for him the rest of his life, why would he want you here now?"

"Because he means something to me!"

"If he meant something to you, you wouldn't

have left!"

"You made me leave!"

Dianne cracked and slapped Aiko. "Don't you know anything, you idiot?"

Quiet.

"If a girl leaves you like that, or if it ends like that, you're supposed to go after her. You aren't supposed to let her raise your kid by herself. You aren't supposed to make girls fall in love with you and then just leave! I never wanted you to leave!"

By this point, Sam was out of the room. He wasn't sure whether to be angry or sad or if he should leave or stay. He wasn't the only confused one in the hallway.

"Then what did you want from me?"

"I..."

Quiet.

"I just wanted to know you cared."

Quiet.

Aiko heard the door close behind him as Sam exited. A sense of relief washed over him. And the next thing Dianne knew, the lips she had fallen in love with eighteen years ago were hers again.

If Jace were awake, he would laugh. This shit is why soap operas existed.

His hands held her face close to his own, and it was like they were in the south again with Bing Crosby music playing in the background. Except the music was Jace's heartbeat monitor.

Beep. Beep. Beep.

Beep. Beep. Beep.

Earl the trucker could still hear the beeps. And when they became louder all of a sudden, he realized the door had opened. The nice man from earlier emerged, and sat.

Sam Sierze made an awkward noise as he sat. It was something of a laugh and a shaky sigh. "I think my fiancé just got back together with her ex-husband from eight years ago."

"Ooh, sorry, buddy. I know the feeling."

"Really?"

"Nope. Just tryin' to make you feel better."

Earl sighed. "I'll... Go get you some coffee."

Sam sighed.

Aiko sighed as he pulled away from Dianne's lips.

Beep. Beep. Beep.

"Why did you leave?" She whispered, tears coming down her face.

Beep. Beep. Beep.

"I've missed you so much."

Beep... Beep... Beep...

It took Aiko and Dianne a couple of seconds to realize that something was happening. Something that wasn't supposed to be happening was happening. Aiko scurried over to his son's bedside, while Dianne froze where she stood. The whole room was an emotional tornado.

Beep...

"Jace?" Dianne whispered, horrified.

Beep...

Aiko Ken Anderson began to panic. His son was dying. His son was lying there with an oxygen mask over his face, which was swollen and battered past the point of recognition. His son was dying. And he didn't even know what to do. He didn't know how to prove he was so sorry.

Then, he remembered a song that Jace grew up with. And he began to sing.

> *"Let me call you Sweetheart*
> *I'm in love with you*
> *Let me hear you whisper..."*

Beep... Beep... Beep...

> *"That you love me too."*

Dianne West began to cry.

Beep...

Aiko Ken Anderson began to cry.

Aiko and Dianne would tell that story for years to come. Both felt the same way; when your child's heart stops, or anyone you love that much, your heart stops too.

> *"Keep the love light glowing*
> *In your eyes so blue*
> *Let me call you Sweetheart*
> *I'm in love with you."*

The beeping came to a sudden stop somewhere around the Bing Crosby bridge, but Jace's father powered through. Tears streamed down his face, but they weren't the pretty kind of tears. Aiko may have been a pretty boy, but nobody cried like they did in the movies. Snot ran down from his nose. His whole body shook.

Dianne fell onto the ground and ripped her wedding dress. Dirt and melted snow and blood littered her dress. Now, as she began to cry, her makeup ran with her tears.

The fall of the Anderson family wasn't graceful. Not in the slightest.

But, then again, these tears were not the only that these four walls had seen. People died every day.

Why was it that only tragedy brought people together?

Jace's funeral was small. Aiko did not attend, neither did Sam. Only a few of Jace's school friends made it. Dianne tried inviting Brook Kella Boe, but she had no way of contacting Jace's long lost crush. At this funeral, there were no speeches. There weren't any flowers or handshakes or kisses. There were barely any tears. Everyone was too stunned for that.

Everyone just sat around and wondered what had all gone wrong.

Chapter Thirty Four

June 1st, 2014
10:39am

Oh god. I should've brought May with me. Why didn't I bring May with me?

Peter struggled just to find the power button on the computer at the library. "Kids these days… With their doodads and their thingamabobs and shit… How the hell am I supposed to keep up with it?" He pressed every button on the keyboard and got nothing. He pressed every button on the monitor and got nothing. He pressed every button on the tower and the desktop roared to life.

Later he would regret yelling, "HELL YEAH" in his accomplished excitement, but we'll get to that later. It took him another fifteen minutes to turn the monitor on. About half an hour after first stepping foot in the library, Peter finally arrived at the Google homepage. He began to type.

Search: how to figure out if someone died

Peter was bombarded with results for worried homeowners who thought someone had died in their house. *I really, really should've brought May with me.* He was just looking for some evidence or some proof that Jace Aiko Anderson had not died. Peter had never heard of a case where someone came back from the dead. He wasn't sure if he believed in angels and he wasn't sure if he believed in God. But he believed, with all of his heart, that Jace wouldn't do this. He wouldn't pull this awful, awful prank. . Not without some reasonable motive.

Search: Teenager dies

Now that just wasn't helpful in the slightest.

Articles from all over the world popped up; Australia, Washington, Scotland, some horror movie reviews, almost everywhere except Clara Barton Hospital. He wracked his brain for the full name of the kid. Jace... Jace was the first name. I just need to remember the last name.

He tried Andrews and nothing came up.

He tried Sanderson and nothing came up.

He tried Anderson and it was like all of his prayers were suddenly answered. In the images portion below the search bar appeared a picture of his daughter's boyfriend; floppy hair, dumb smile and everything. He held his high school diploma and his graduation cap was crooked. Peter would expect nothing less from Jace. A Facebook profile popped up, with him and his dog as the profile picture.

Jace led a life that was similar to how Peter pictured it; he volunteered at a chess camp and had dogs and loved his mom. He posted dumb little quotes from poetry books and movies and liked to talk about what he would do after graduation. He wanted to fly helicopters, but he was told he would never get to do that, so he wanted to go into coding.

Peter continued to scroll, out of curiosity. Finally, he found a column on the side that said "related groups."

Dog lovers.

Chess players.

Rest in Peace Jace Aiko Anderson.

Peter's heart stopped. It seemed there was no difference between Jace and Peter now.

"Oh god." It took a couple of intense moments before Peter Boe clicked on the link. He didn't even want to; he had his proof. He could just print out this one page and be done with it. But his curiosity got the best of him and he selected the link.

"I miss u so much man. U were the gr8est. r i p"

"Jace was one of the kindest people I ever knew. I wish he wasn't gone. My heart goes out to his family."

"A funeral will be held for Jace Aiko Anderson in the park closest to the school. Please feel free to come; I'm sure he would've wanted all of you there." That post was made by a woman named Dianne West. Who was Dianne West?

Alright, so he's dead. Now how did he die? How is he even here? What the hell is happening? Peter's head spun around and around and around. It was insane. All of this was insane. This mystery boy shows up to his daughter's hotel room, with bouquets of roses day in and day out, and a stuffed Nemo toy. How would he even know about the whole Nemo thing? And Brooke barely remembered his name, why would he go out of his way to come and visit her? How was he visiting her when he was dead? Maybe there was just another Jace Aiko Anderson who happened to go to Casimir Pulaski High School, and died on January first.

Peter went back to the search engine page.

Search: Jace Anderson dies

Sparse were the results, but one in particular caught his eye.

High School Graduate Dies in Fatal Car Crash on New Year's Day.

Oh god.

"Jace Anderson, a recent graduate at Casimir Pulaski High School, had been driving his mother, Dianne West, and her fiance to their wedding in a nearby park. This was when tragedy struck. Earl Koski had been driving his semi pickup truck when the two cars collided. Koski called 911 and Anderson was found with several broken bones and a punctured lung. West and her fiancé, Sam Sierze, only sustained mild injuries."

Below the article was a picture that must've been taken minutes before they left in the car. Jace was wearing a light blue button up shirt with a dark green jacket.

It was the same thing Jace would wear every day to visit Brooke.

"Anderson passed away hours later in Clara Barton Hospital, surrounded by his family. 'Our community has lost a bright spark,' West commented, the most beautiful boy you could ever imagine, really.' Jace Anderson was a chess coach and also wanted to go into computer coding when he got older. He will be missed."

Oh god. Oh god oh god oh god ohgodohgodohgod. What am I going to tell Brooke? Peter frantically tried to figure out how to print the one page and wandered around to find a printer. Everything's so damn complicated. He had to pay for every page he printed; ten cents per colored page. He threw a handful of change at the stuffy looking librarian, turned on his heel, and ran faster than he ever had before.

Jace, meanwhile, sat out in the park where his funeral was held. He had no reason to be back here on this stupid planet anymore. He had messed everything up and he could accept that.

Now he just wanted to go back to being dead in peace.

But he began to think about Brooke. Would she live? Had he done enough for her? He hoped he had held her enough times and kissed her enough times to transfer the energy he had intended. Brooke Kella Boe would most likely live. She probably would've if Jace wasn't there, he liked to believe. She was so stubborn. No cancer would kick her ass without her permission, that was for sure.

He rubbed his right cheek. It still stung and Jace suspected that wouldn't stop anytime soon. Everything hurt. The park, though, brought him some comfort. *Where's Mom now? I wonder if her and Sam ever got married. I hope they did, he really liked her. Am I allowed to go find out?*

Jace stood carefully, like someone would get mad at him for moving too fast or something. He took careful steps toward his house, 288 Moore Street. *What if she wasn't there? What if she moved?* His house was only a few blocks away from the park...

But when he arrived there, he wasn't even sure if he wanted to enter. The door was left open. That's really bad, he thought. That's so bad. Jace stepped in as quietly as he could.

Yelling erupted from the living room. "You're just going to leave again?"

"I left because you made me, Dianne! I don't want to be around. You have a fiancé and Jace is gone and there's no reason for me to stay here anymore."

Jace's whole world came to a stop. He recognized that voice, from the moments he was being born and the moments he was dying.

"Dad?"

Chapter Thirty Five

June 1st, 2014:
11:00am

Peter ran as fast as he could from the library back to Clara Barton Hospital. It was almost two and a half miles, and he could've called a taxi, but with the downtown traffic it would've done him no good.

He would be exhausted after this was all over. Hell, he was exhausted now. He was so exhausted that he thought he saw Jace on the street, running to his own destination. Peter took a double take, but Jace was nowhere to be seen.

Peter came to the next and final stop in his journey; the front desk of Clara Barton Hospital. The girl with the headphones still sat there, scrolling through some social networking site probably.

"Hey, you," he searched for a name tag, "Jackie. Was there ever a patient named Jason Anderson here? Shit, I mean Jace Anderson."

She didn't answer, she just typed frantically. "I... Yes, there was." Emphasis on the past tense.

"When did he die?"

"He died on January first, 2014."

"How old was he?"

"Eighteen, sir. Did you know him?" Jackie could remember almost perfectly, the day that Jace was brought in on a stretcher. It was her second day of work. She had been so mad that she had to work on New Year's, and was exhausted from staying up all night the night before. She put on a playlist of loud hip hop to keep herself awake, as it was a relatively quiet day. Her boyfriend came to visit her, coincidentally, a few minutes before Jace came in the doors. He brought her a bouquet of purple flowers.

Peter couldn't be bothered to answer her question. He flew down the hallway and to the stairwell. Sweat ran down the side of his forehead, and down his neck. *I hate running, he thought. I was on track team and I hate running.*

Fourth floor.

Room four hundred and thirty three.

Four.

Three.

Three.

He burst through the door to find it unusually clean. The rose petals had been swept up and disposed of, Brooke's blood wasn't on the sheets, and Brooke was sitting on the bed. It looked so much better, and it made Peter relax just a little bit.

"Hey, D-dad..." Brooke murmured. She was still pretty shook up, despite her clean appearance. Her eyes remained red and she looked more fragile than she ever had before. Even so, upon seeing him, Brooke leapt up from the bed. "What happened to you?"

"I... You... Here, I need to go get some coffee." Shit was getting too weird for Peter Boe. He handed his daughter the folded, crumpled article from the internet. "I'll get you some too." He hurried out just as fast as he had come in. Peter always considered himself good at being there for his daughter, but he had no idea how Brooke would react and he was still trying to figure out how he was reacting. May wasn't anywhere to be seen.

Brooke's nose wrinkled up in confusion. The paper, folded up and crumpled, was slightly damp. She was almost afraid to open it, when Peter left, like she was alone with a criminal or a crook. It took her a while to decide to open it, finally. She held Eeyore in her arms as she did.

"Local Teenager Dies In Fatal Car Accident."

Peter came back with three cups of coffee. He needed two for himself; one for now and one for later. He figured, if he stopped moving, he wouldn't want to get up again. *My body wasn't built for spontaneous four mile runs.*

He set the three cups on the windowsill near his chair blanket fort. *No audible crying or screaming, that's good. She must be okay. I don't know how she's okay, because I am sure as hell not okay.*

"This is some weird shit we're getting into, Brooke." Peter began to rub Brooke's back, then handed her a cup of coffee.

Hunched over the article, Peter didn't know if she was crying or not. Her pointer finger followed the words, a particular phrase, over and over again.

Jace Aiko Anderson.

Jace Aiko Anderson.

Jace Aiko Anderson.

"I know," Peter murmured, "I know, it's hard."

How could he know? Brooke said nothing. She thought nothing and felt nothing and did nothing. The article was a black hole that sucked out any motivation she had, for anything. "I really..." choking, Brooke Kella Boe looked up at her father, "I really m-messed up, huh?" There wasn't any other way to word it. Brooke brought this boy down from wherever the afterlife was and made him stay for a month, then sent him away. *Why wouldn't I believe him? Has he ever lied to me before? Well, yes. He told me he had a job, for one. But...*

"It's not your fault, sweetheart. How were you supposed to know?"

"But how could I assume that he was lying?"

"Don't beat yourself up over this, Brooke. You've gotta find a way to fix it."

"And how the hell would you suggest I did that?"

Peter was startled by her choice of vocabulary. "I don't know. But I do know that you're the smartest girl on the face of the planet and that you'll figure something out.

She would never figure it out.

Chapter Thirty Six

June 1st, 2014
12:50am

Jace slapped his hands over his mouth after realizing what he had done; first his right hand, then his left.

But his father, nor his mother, responded.

"I can't stay here, Dianne. You have a whole other world and so do I."

"So, what? You think you can come in here and kiss me and stay a couple months and leave?" Dianne responded almost sarcastically. "I'm not losing you again. I promised I would never lose you again and you promised you would never leave again." *I've lost way too much,* she thought.

After she lost the baby in the accident, she began to lose her mind.

Jace's eyebrows jumped a few inches up on his forehead. "Wait, can't you guys hear me?" He took a few more steps into the house, and into the living room. The couple wasn't in there, though, they were in the dining room. Something shattered.

"But my whole family is in Florida, Dianne. I have to go back to them."

"The last time you left, our son had to grow up with a mother making minimum wage and he ended up passing away because you weren't there for him."

"Don't you dare blame me for this."

"Why not? It's your fault."

Dianne and Aiko knew each other for a long time, but this was the first time Dianne could ever remember hearing the strong and silent man raise his voice. And it was utterly terrifying.

"Let me tell you something. *You* made me leave. *You* thought I was a bad influence on him. And I wasn't around, and now he's dead. If you tell me one more time that it was my fault, I will turn around and walk out right now."

Quiet.

Quiet.

Jace stood in the doorway, but neither of them acknowledged him. He was sorta happy for this; he didn't want his dad to see him cry.

Dianne repeated, "It's your fault." She only said it because she didn't believe him. Aiko was just bluffing. He was a bad liar, just like his son.

"I'm sorry, Dianne." Aiko had decided, right then and there, that it was time to make decisions based on what he wanted. "I'm going home."

"This is your home."

"I wish it was."

Jace began to breakdown. "No, don't go. She's lost without you. She's just- You know she isn't the best at trying to say the right thing. I'm not either! Just stay. Please. I know it's confusing to see me and I know it'll freak you out but I don't want to watch you walk away from her again!" He took a single heroic step between his father and the dining room doorway.

But when Aiko pushed past towards the front door, it wasn't what Jace expected. He might've expected a cliché moment where Aiko just walked through Jace, like the ghost he was. But, instead, Jace would just disappear and reappear on the other side of the doorway.

I've run out of time.

"I've run out of time."

This realization hit him like a ton of bricks to the face. He turned to his mother and grabbed her shoulders, shaking her, "I can't run out of time!"

Dianne did nothing.

Jace became desperate. He swung his fist at his mother, trying to get her attention in any way he could and failing. A small vase with water and dead flowers sat on the table and he had an idea. It probably wasn't a very good idea but it was an idea nonetheless. He picked up the glass vase and threw it. It hit the wall and shattered, much to Jace's delight. "Please, just pay attention to me!"

Startled, Aiko span around to face his ex-wife. "Did you just throw that at me?"

"Throw what?"

"The vase."

"No... No, I didn't."

"That's really mature, Dianne. Way to be an adult," Aiko sarcastically grumbled. And with that, he walked out the door.

In Jace's attempt to help, he just drove his father away faster. He just drove his mother into the deeper hole of loneliness. Sam was gone. Sam left that day at the hospital. He gathered his things and never returned to Moore Street. Dianne hoped he was happy; he deserved it. He just didn't come in at the right time.

Dianne glanced at the broken glass on the floor. She didn't clean it up. She just sat at a chair nearby and tried to figure out how it'd happened. Maybe she did throw it and she didn't even realize it. Am I losing my mind?

Jace sighed. He took in a big breath of air, let it out, and still felt as empty as he did before. A seat was open next to his mother, and he took it. "I'm sorry, Mom. That was kinda my fault, huh? Now you're lonely and I'm lonely and he's lonely... " Lonely was the theme here and he hated it.

No answer. Not like he expected one, though. It just felt nice to talk.

"It was totally my fault. I just... Got mad. I knew this would happen, though. They told me I would only have a certain amount of time when I came down, and I always meant to visit you... I just never knew when the right time was. And now this girl - you know, Brooke? The one you wanted me to ask to prom? Anyway - she's in the hospital and she probably hates me with all of her guts. Ha, oops. That's my fault too, though. I'm just so good at messing things up, huh?"

Quiet. Dianne began to cry.

"I only had a certain amount of time down here and I used it the best I could. Now, I'm stuck here. I'm a ghost, or something. I don't know what to do with myself; do I go to stranger's houses and push books off of shelves? Should I make people think their houses are haunted? Should I save people? I can't go home. I don't want to go home. Because..."

Dianne jerked her head up and gave Jace the smallest glimmer of hope that she could hear him. But it was just in response to the thunder off in the distance.

Her head returned to her hands and tears streamed from her eyes, down her arms and to the floor.

"Mom, what do I do?"

Quiet. Except for the cat, who purred underneath the couch.

"Mom, please."

Nothing.

"I'm so lost, Mom. You're the only one I can turn to. I screwed up big time, and..." Jace laughed apologetically, "I really, really wanna fix it. And you're the best fixer upper I know. You're the best person at fixing things. You would really like Brooke's dad. He would like to say that he was 'a master in screwing up, and therefore a master in fixing things' and that's what you've always said. Why am I even talking to you? You can't hear me. This was entirely useless and what I did didn't make the slightest difference in Brooke's life and she didn't need me and she never needed me and I'm such a piece of shit and I'm so dependent on other people... Or I was, I was dependent on other people. How did you guys stand me? I rant and I bicker and she would kiss me to shut me up. You guys could never do that." His pace increased. He didn't know that a ghost, a pure soul, could feel nervous or anxious. "It's just all bullshit, you know? You shouldn't be alone and I shouldn't be dead and none of this worked out the way I wanted it to..."

It became harder and harder for Jace to listen to his mother's sobs. He began to cry himself. Could a ghost cry?

"I'll just go."

Jace Aiko Anderson slowly stood from the wooden chair, in the dining room where he grew up. He took a few minutes to walk around, from room to room.

His room was exactly the way he had left it; down to the DVDs sitting out and the half-finished chess game he had started with one of his students over a year ago. The bed wasn't made and Dianne always got mad at him for not making the bed, but he was always too lazy in the mornings. His tennis shoes sat underneath the bed and everything was covered in a mixture of dog hair and dust.

It was weirdly comforting. It was nice to know that some things really don't change; not as much as it seems like they do. Maybe I could just stay here, he thought. I could just keep mom company. I could write in the dust and move stuff around... But that might just scare her away.

The guest room was locked. Jace found the key, on the top of the door frame, and opened the door. This room had also sat, untouched, since the day Jace passed away and the day Dianne West should've become Mrs. Dianne West Sierze.

The wedding dress.

The wedding dress was crumpled up and thrown on the bed. No one had even washed it. It was covered, drenched in water stains and makeup and blood. Jace often thought about how hard it must've been for his mother. She lost two important men and gained one and then lost him again. She didn't have any siblings and her parents had passed away in some assisted living home somewhere in Nevada, having totally forgot about their only daughter out of five children.

Jace never really considered how hard her entire life must have been.

Everyone's life was so hard.

Earl's life was hard. How could he live with killing some eighteen year old boy on his mother's wedding day?

Brooke's life was hard, but she would never admit it.

May's life was hard, and maybe part of that was her fault and maybe part of it wasn't.

Life is just so hard. Jace had been relieved of his duties on January first, in Clara Barton Hospital in room three hundred and one. It was a weird thing to be grateful for, definitely. But in the same weird way, he was grateful. Life was one of the hardest things he ever experienced and he only got one fourth of his allotted time.

Dying is easy. Living is hard.

Maybe that's why Brooke would stay alive. She was never one to take the easy way out.

Chapter Thirty Seven

February 29th, 2016
1:29pm

"Did anything come in the mail for me today, Dad?"

"Yep."

"What is it?"

"You mean, what are they?"

"I got two? Give 'em!"

Peter held the two letters over his head for his daughter to try to reach. Brooke laughed, hopping on one foot with her hands up.

"Just give them to me!"

"What do we say?"

"Now!"

"Brooke! Be nice. I know that I taught you better manners than that."

She groaned. "Please, can I have my letters?"

"I don't know, can you?"

If looks could kill, Peter Boe would've died right then.

"Sure, fine." Peter surrendered and handed his daughter the two letters.

Jace liked to linger around the Boe residence. "I know what they are! I know, I know!"

"Dad, where's the letter opener?"

"I dunno. Do I look like I ever know where anything is, Brooke?"

Brooke bounded around in her excitement. Jace loved being around her and watching her grow. She was no longer the tiny girl from hospital room four hundred and thirty three. She was no longer losing her hair and she was no longer confined to the mattress of a hospital mattress. Brooke Kella Boe had always been strong, but now it was visible. "I know where it is, Nemo. C'mon, it's in the drawer next to the sink." He bounded around the two in the kitchen, skipping on bare feet. He could not open the drawer and hand the letter opener to his beloved. He could only knock on the wooden drawer to call her attention to it.

"Do you think they'll accept you?"

"Stanford won't. I applied there because you dared me to."

"So what do I get if you get accepted?"

She rolled her eyes then sighed. "You... Get something. I don't know. I'll decide later. Besides, they didn't accept me anyway so it doesn't matter."

"Right, right. Just open it, Jesus."

His daughter laughed. She heard something shift in the drawer by the sink so she opened it and retrieved the letter opener. "Here, found it." Brooke's heart beat hard in her chest. She slid the razor along the inside of the envelope. Everything could change after this, she thought. The letter read:

"Dear Brooke Kella Boe,

We are excited to inform you that you have been accepted into Stanford's Architectural Design program with a full scholarship. Enclosed is registration instructions. Thank you for applying and we hope to see you in the fall!"

There was more to the letter, of course, but that was all Brooke really cared about. "I can't believe it."

Peter perched himself over her shoulder. "I knew it. You owe me."

"What on earth could I owe you?"

"You have to help me bring in firewood, and I don't have to pay you for it this time."

Jace wanted so badly to embrace Brooke. He wanted to hug her and tell her how wonderful he thought she was. But the time for that was long gone, and Jace needed to accept that. It was just a lot harder than he ever thought it would be. "Wow, Brooke! I always told you that you were smart." He followed her around like a duckling following around his mother duck. He would run and try to move things so she wouldn't trip. Jace's whole existence, at this point, was dedicated to her, and it was how he liked it.

Oh my god. What is mom gonna say? She'll be so happy... What would Jace say?

"Hey, dad?" Brooke sounded very sheepish all of a sudden.

"Yeah, Nemo?" Peter got his wood gloves on.

"Do you think Jace would be proud of me?"

Peter knew better than anyone that Brooke still wasn't entirely over what happened with Jace Aiko Anderson. Hell, he was still pretty confused himself and doubted it would ever be cleared up in his lifetime. But he was weirdly okay with that. "I'm gonna answer your question with another question. Do *you* think Jace would be proud of you, Brooke?"

Quiet.

Thoughtful silence.

"I think he'd be proud of me... Really proud, actually. Don't you think?"

"I don't know. He was your boyfriend, not mine."

"He wasn't my boyfriend, Dad."

Jace made a weird noise that sounded like a snort and a laugh. "Stop lying to yourself, Brooke."

Peter, ironically, murmured the same thing at the same time. Eerily, it sounded to Brooke like two people were saying it. "Now what does the other one say?"

The second letter had no return address. In fact, it had no address at all. It just said Brooke's full name in poorly practiced cursive. It looked like someone slaved over it though, like they had too much time on their hands and just wanted to make her something nice. Jace, again, came to mind. I hate when he does that. So, Brooke didn't answer. "Let's just go out and get the wood, okay?"

Her father just raised an eyebrow but returned his gaze back to his gloves. "Alright. C'mon, Nemo. We got work to do."

Half an hour passed by, and out of those eighteen hundred seconds, she was thinking about the letter for at least one thousand, six hundred and fifty five of those seconds. Possibly one thousand, six hundred and fifty six. It would depend on what you would count as thinking about the letter.

Around one thousand, two hundred and three, Brooke dropped a piece of wood on her foot because she was thinking about the letter.

Or maybe not the letter, but Jace.

After three bandages and a bloody foot, Brooke was done with the wood and ready to read the mysterious letter. And Peter let her go willingly. He needed to call May and see what she was up to, anyway.

But she threw it under the bed instead.

Chapter Thirty Eight

August 9th, 2016
8:00pm

"Will you marry me?"

Brooke just stared at him. Not even at him, really, but off into space above his head. Nothing came to mind. She had no idea what to say to the man on one knee. Traditionally, someone would answer with yes or no. Traditional was never the first word that sprang to Brooke's mind.

Her eyes met his, and she blurted out what she was thinking in panic. "I don't know!" A weight lifted off her chest. "I... Sorry. But I really don't know."

The sad look in his eyes panicked her more than the actual question. "Oh..." He stood up and closed the tiny, navy blue velvet box. "Yeah. I understand." He wasn't that surprised but he also wasn't happy.

"I mean, I really like you! But..."

"You don't know."

"Right. I really don't know. I'm really sorry."

"It's okay. Really, it's fine."

"It's not fine. I promise I'll have an answer for you tomorrow. Just meet me in the park."

"Okay... Do you want me to drive you home?"

"No. I can walk." Brooke kissed his cheek, trying to make it less awkward for them both but ultimately failing.

Twenty one years old, attending university for a Master's in architecture, but still living with her mother and father because they needed her, Brooke Kella Boe was right where she needed to be. And a wedding didn't seem very... Practical.

Not even getting married to a twenty three year old with a degree in engineering and a minor in chemistry, whose name was Jason Austin Grey. Her and ason started dating two years ago after they met in a coffee shop. How cliché, right?

Brooke began her short trek home. The awkward, embarrassment didn't wear off, even as she got further away. She left in the middle of their dessert. *I should've at least taken that piece of cake, damn it.*

Jason was working at the Starbucks on the corner. Brooke never went there and almost went out of her way to avoid it; she saw a lot of her old classmates and current classmates. She didn't like seeing people in the first place, she wasn't a morning person and she sure as hell didn't like seeing people in the morning. And then you add on the fact that she hasn't eaten anything, has her hair up in a lazy ponytail and is wearing sweatpants...

Yeah, Brooke didn't like mornings. At all.

Jason, on the other hand, was a total morning person. Just like Jace, she would later realize. But that was the only thing they had in common; Jason had a built form and blonde, straight hair and bright eyes. He wasn't clumsy, he didn't talk too much, he was perfectly coordinated for his size.

Plus, he was good at math.

Brooke brushed her winter boots off on the welcome mat. "I'm home!"

No response. She didn't expect one, though. Peter liked his naps at night and May liked getting work done before she came home. *Good, I won't be bothered.*

She needed nothing more than to think.

In her room, on the second story of 288 Moore Street, Brooke Kella Boe collapsed onto her queen sized bed.

"Ugh, why?" Groaning, she rolled over onto her back.

Why did Jason have to propose? Why did she have to go and be weird about it? Why didn't she just break up with him earlier if she didn't see a future with him? *Why? Why why why why why? Why am I still obsessed with that floppy haired, golden voiced idiot? He's dead.*

Brooke, he's dead.

He is literally dead.

Just marry Jason and move on already.

Brooke shoved her palms into her eyes, until she began to see the little stars and galaxies in her mind. She began to repeat to herself:

"Oh shut up. Every time it rains, it stops raining. Every time you hurt, you heal. After darkness, there is always light and you get reminded of this every morning but still you choose to believe that the night will last forever. Nothing lasts forever. Not the good or the bad. So you might as well smile while you're here."

"Smile. Smile. Smile."

"Just keep swimming."

Brooke heard Jace's voice in her head, with the stars and galaxies. Maybe he never really existed, and everyone just humored her in her delusions. But then where did all the roses come from? Where did the letter come from?

The letter.

The letter!

"Oh god, where did I put it?" *I can't ever keep track of things. What if I left it in the old house?*

This single thought prompted a scavenger hunt into the deepest depths of Brooke's bedroom; under high school yearbooks and laundry baskets and desks. She practically cleared her bookshelf for nothing. "Oh god."

Brooke pulled a family portrait off the wall. The letter was not hidden behind there. It was not hidden behind the framed Finding Nemo concept art that Peter got her for her eighteenth birthday. It was not behind her framed high school diploma and consequenting college acceptance letter. "Oh god, oh god." *Did I just imagine it?*

Panic overcame her whole body. Dropping to the floor, she looked underneath the bed.

And there it was.

Still sealed; never opened.

Covered in dust.

Written on with a really cheap pen, and cursive strokes that must've been traced over thousands of times by the original author. Brooke had no proof that this letter was from her Jace Aiko Anderson. She had never opened it. She was too afraid to. But now, now felt like the right time.

And Jace was there. "Jesus, it's only been three years. I thought you would forget about it." He sat in the corner, cross legged. "Are you really gonna marry that guy? He kinda seems like a square. Don't get me wrong, I love people. But people have told me I'm the jealous type. Not like I could do anything about you marrying him. You'll just have to get a puppy that I can play with while you're banging him in the bedroom."

The knick knacks on Brooke's shelf were occasionally rearranged while she wasn't paying attention. This was one of Jace's favorite hobbies.

Brooke couldn't open it. She just... Stared at it.

"C'mon, the suspense is literally killing me. Literally. Brooke, I'm dead," Jace flopped over onto her bed and laughed. He made himself laugh. He had to keep upbeat; he estimated his stay for about another eighty years.

Over the last three years, Jace had learned how to float, communicate with the living and make things invisible. He liked to call himself Danny Phantom and knew Brooke would call him ridiculous for this. But, for now, he just flicked the envelope.

The envelope flinched right in front of Brooke's eyes. She almost threw it, whispering, "I'm losing my mind."

"At least you still have one. I really miss mine. I

haven't had one since, like... Sixth grade? I don't know. Whenever my parents got me a Wii, that was when my mental capacity went downhill. Dude, we never played *Super Smash Brothers* together! When you die, we'll figure out how to play it. I mean, if you die. Modern medicine is a weird thing."

Brooke took out a maroon pocket knife, her MacGyver-ish letter opener, and hesitated once more.

"Jesus, Brooke! I don't even remember what I wrote, open it already."

She seemed to hear his sentence as she immediately tore it open.

"Hey, be gentle, I worked my ass off on that cursive. Not like I had anything better to do, or anything."

She seemed to hear this as well. Brooke closed the knife and set it down on the carpet. She re-positioned herself, sitting criss cross applesauce on her floor, like she did when she would study. "Oh god."

Brooke pulled it out of the envelope.

Seconds felt like hours for Jace. "Brooke, seriously! Now you're the ridiculous one." His sarcasm hid his concern. He didn't know why he still faked emotions; there was really no need to, no one saw him anyway. But he had never been good at expressing himself anyway. Why should he start after death?

He was concerned for her. Would it hurt her, to read what he wrote two and a half years ago? Would it hold her back from getting married to what's his name? "I just... I want you to be happy. I'm pretty sure I wrote that somewhere, but I really mean it." Jace took the same position she did, criss cross applesauce, right across from her, so he could watch her face.

Her beautiful, strong face. Could a face be strong? "I'm so bad at describing things. But you're about to see that in a second, too."

And, finally, Brooke began to read.

"Dear Brooke,

Hey. Umm... I don't know where to start. I'm writing in pen and I really haven't thought any of this out so just bear with me here, alright?

I'm sorry. I'm so sorry.

I'm truly, very, deeply sorry. With every part of me that still exists. I should've told you. I probably shouldn't have even come down in the first place. It was really... What's the word? Self absorbed of me. I didn't think about what would happen when I told you or when I had to leave.

But I didn't think you'd fall in love with me, either.

I didn't really think you needed my help.

And you really didn't.

I guess I just wanted an excuse to come down and help you. You deserve as much time on your feet as you can get.

Selfish! Selfish was the word I was looking for earlier. I was being selfish. I need a thesaurus or something, I'm terrible at writing.

Umm..."

A couple words were scribbled out, past the point of recognition. A tear fell from Brooke's eye and to the floor.

"You mean so much to me. You always have. You always will. I've been in love with you from the first moment I saw you, with your twin braids. You're literally the most stubborn person I know, and it's absolutely insane. I love it. I love you. I can't even put it into words. I want to be a poet for you, and write about rivers and trees and compare you to the prettiest thing on the planet but I'm really bad at that. I'm not a writer. I'm not good at math, either. I'm not good at very much anything, it seems. I've never really... Found my purpose.

But, as cliché as it sounds, I found my purpose when I died. After I died. I died and went to some... Weird place. It's not a heaven, or a hell. I'm really not sure what it is. I hope you won't have to find out for a long, long time.

I died and I went to this weird place, but I could still see you. I watched you in that hospital bed for months before I came down there. It was nice to just watch you. Is that weird? I wasn't watching you the whole time. I gave you your privacy, I swear. I'm not that weird. Wow, I just need to shut up."

Jace laughed. "Yep, I did. I still do."

"I don't remember where I was going with this. I just needed to write you something. I'm still here. I'm with you. You'll hear little knocks on wood and leaves shuffling behind you when you walk home. And you should know; it's just me. I want to watch over you for the rest of your life. Then, after that maybe, we can talk some more. We can watch Finding Nemo in whatever that weird place was. But until then, I'm not going there without you. I belong with you. I feel complete with you. You could be your tiny self or a giant European man with a burly mustache and I would still probably like you as much. You mean so much to me. Infinitely, but more than that. Infinitely times ten. And that's why I'll always be with you."

Brooke knew it was from him; it wasn't some fake letter. She knew it was from him because it was written in his voice, with the same ranting stupidity that she missed so much.

"I'm probably with you right now. Do

something. I'll do something back."

Now this just sort of scared her. Did ghosts really exist? Was he a poltergeist?

Peter had said one time, in the hospital, "This is some weird shit we're getting into." And Brooke couldn't agree more.

She still had to try.

She took the envelope that originally contained the letter, crumpled it up in her hand, and threw it towards the window.

"Oh, right. I should be paying attention, huh?" Jace leapt up from his spot, grabbing the envelope. It didn't hit the window.

Brooke only saw it stop in mid air.

Jace slowly brought it back to her, uncrumpled it and set it next to her crossed legs. "What did I tell you, Brooke? We'll be in our fifties and I'll remember your name. Well, you'll be in your fifties, at least."

"Jace? Can you hear me?"

"Yeah, it's me." It hurt him so much. She couldn't hear him and he knew it.

Jace wanted to resume his position across from her, but she was crying. He could barely stand to see her cry, especially when he was crying himself. "I'm sorry, Brooke." He didn't know what he was sorry for. He didn't know what to say.

Brooke followed the envelope with her bright eyes, until it landed on the floor and uncrumpled itself. I don't know if I should believe it, she thought. "God damn it, Jace, why... Why can't you go home? Just go home!"

Jace sighed, thinking about how to phrase his sentences. "Nope. I need you. You don't need me but I sure as hell need you, and you're not getting rid of me that easily. Plus I can't go back, but that's not the point." It was ironic, he had a filter after being quiet for so long. It gave him time to think.

The guy at the end of Inception really did live.

He solved a Rubix cube.

He organized all of the books in the library by author, then title, then color. And he constantly wondered what the librarians thought of that.

But now, Jace Aiko Anderson needed to figure out a way to communicate with her. Nothing came to mind immediately. The room didn't have that much in it, besides textbooks and swimsuits and framed diplomas. There was a large marker under her bookshelf, and Jace squeezed himself under it to retrieve the black marker.

Now, I just need something to write on. Not the letter... The envelope's crumbled.

Ah, screw it.

After yelling into her empty room, Brooke broke into tears. She cried quietly, and it really freaked Jace out.

"You cry like a super villain, I swear to god. I feel like you're gonna jerk your head up and your eyes are going to be glowing red or something weird like that." Jace shut his lips, and bit the lower one while he concentrated. He forgot how to write over two years.

Brooke cried and cried and cried. *Stop crying. Stop crying. Stop crying.* She repeated it over and over in her head. *Stop it. There's no reason for you to be crying. This happened so long ago... It doesn't matter anymore. Just go marry Jason.*

And that was when she noticed Jace writing on her hand.

Chapter Thirty Nine

May 30th, 2014
6:26pm

"I've always just wanted you to be happy." Jace blurted.

"What?"

"Yeah. I think you're really neat and you're even neater when you're happy."

Jace sat with his arm around her, in their rebuilt blanket fort. "That's why I'm here."

"I thought you were here because you thought I was lonely."

"... That too. But really because I like being around you."

"Why?"

"Why? Um... I don't know. It's hard to explain."

"Try."

"Uh... You're very stubborn. You're introverted. You don't talk a lot. You speak for yourself. And you're so ridiculously smart. I can't put my finger on it, really. I've had a crush on you for a really," Jace pecked her cheek, "really," then her nose, "really," and he finally kissed her lips. "Really long time."

She rubbed her lips together. Jace could tell she was thinking, and wanted to say something but was wondering if she really should say it. "Just say it."

Brooke groaned. "I hate when you do that."

"What?"

"Read my mind."

Jace twisted his face, obviously offended. "When have I ever done that?"

"I don't know… Only, like, every day since you've started visiting me. How did you know my favorite color was purple? And I don't ever remember telling you about the whole Nemo thing."

"How could you not have told me about it? You doodled Nemo on my papers when you were bored. I got points docked off of my homework for it, just so you know. It's a miracle that I passed that class sitting next to you."

"Whatever," she grumbled, playing with her hands. She had this bad habit of picking at her fingernails, just when she didn't have anything better to do. "I don't even remember what we were talking about now. Thanks a lot." Brooke pushed her lower lip out and crinkled up her nose.

This was the beginning of one of their games. It was called the "how fast can Jace make Brooke laugh when she's trying really hard not to laugh" game. It was Jace's favorite game and Brooke's least favorite game.

"Hey, stop making that face at me. You're not really grumpy."

"Who says I'm not really grumpy?"

"Me. I can tell when you're really grumpy, Grumpy Pants."

"How would you be able to tell?"

"You said it yourself."

"What?"

"I like to read your mind."

"Yeah? Well then, what's my mind saying right now?"

Jace had something clever in his mind. It was clever and it was flirty and he had the balls to say it. *I won't mess it up, I won't mess it up, I won't mess it up.* He wanted to say, "I know what will be on your mind in a few moments." And then she would say, "what?" And he would deliver the final flirt by saying, "kissing me," and kissing her! It was genius. *I got this.*

"I know what you'll be kissing in a few moments."

Crap. Damn. Crap. Damn. Kill me now. I'm already dead. Re-kill me. Bury me under this hospital.

Jace awaited her response. It was almost the scariest thing he ever experienced.
And finally, she just wrinkled up her nose. "What?"

"What? Nothing. Pfft. I didn't say anything, duh."

"Did you just try to flirt with me?"

"Nuh uh. Nope. You're imagining things. I didn't say anything."

"You're such a bad liar. What did you even say?"

"Nothing!" Jace was almost sweating by now. "It was just me, being an idiot. You get to see that all the time."

"Okay okay, what were you trying to say?"

This was why she wanted him around. He, in the eyes of the state, was an adult. And she was pretty damn close. But, here they were, sitting in a blanket fort made of mostly pink sheets and watching Disney film after Disney film. Right now, it was *Nightmare Before Christmas*. They were adults. Adults wrapped up in big sheets and making dumb jokes.

Jace was bright red. He was so embarrassed. Oh, god. "No, it's really dumb. I... I was trying to say that you were gonna be thinking about kissing me because I was gonna kiss you and everything... I was trying to be Prince Eric or something."

"Prince Eric?"

"The... The Prince from *the Little Mermaid*. Are you serious? We're watching that next, after I recover from that earth shattering flirting attempt."

Brooke decided on that moment that she was in love with him. *Him, that idiot.* And she began to laugh. She laughed and she laughed.

Jace thought it was actually kind of scary. Was she laughing at him? Was she losing her mind? Because that could happen sometimes. "Are you, um, laughing at me?"

"No! N-no," she managed through her fits of laughter, "I'm laughing... At you, sorta. But in the best way possible. I just... You're so ridiculous. I love it."

Chapter Forty

August 10th, 2016
8:00am

"I can't marry you."

"You can't marry me?"

"Yeah. Oh, shit, I sound like such a jerk. I just... I don't know what to say or how to explain it. It's just... Like..."

"Wow."

"W-what?"

"I've never seen you speechless. Is something wrong?"

Jason was so nice, and it was so bad. He didn't deserve this weird situation. He was cute and so nice and any girl in this city would be lucky to have him.

And Jace didn't even want Brooke to do this. "Look, I know I said something dumb about Jason, but I didn't mean it! He seems really cool." He swirled around her absent mindedly.

Brooke kept her hands hidden, shoved in her pockets. She couldn't get all of the ink off. "No! No, nothing's wrong. I mean, not really. But I just... Can't marry you, Jason." Brooke kept repeating it and couldn't stop. Having a blabber mouth wasn't normal. "I just can't marry you."

"Okay... So, what now?" Jason was awfully calm about this. He tended to be pretty emotional. "Are we just going to go back to what we did before?"

Jace slapped Brooke's arm. He literally slapped her. Too bad he was a freaking spirit with no sense of feeling or will over the physical world. "Stay with him, damn it! Stay with him and get married and have three kids and a really unorganized house with like five dogs!" He was just yelling to himself. "Yesterday, you seemed to hear me. Hear me now. Please?"

Brooke, solemnly, shook her head. "It's really hard to explain. I'm really sorry."

Jason kept quiet. Unpleasant was the word that kept coming to Brooke's mind.

"No, I get it..."

No, you really don't. Oh, god. I'm such a piece of shit. Brooke screamed internally. *How come I never learned how to express my emotions reasonably? I'll need to work on that.* "Look, I, um... Sorry. I'm just gonna go." She was one hundred percent ready to turn her back, and go back to hiding away in her textbooks for the rest of her life.

"Wait."

"Hm?"

"He's lucky."

Her eyebrow arched up and her nose crinkled up, "what?"

"Whoever has you. He's lucky. And I really hope you're happy with him."

And with that, Jason Austin Grey turned his back away from her and walked off into the park. She would never see him again.

She continued to have her tiny existential crisis long after he was gone. *Why can't I just break up with someone like a normal person? Why can't I have a regular love life with someone who isn't dead? Why? Why can't I just exist? This is all so difficult, damn it Jace.* Brooke rubbed her hands together in an attempt to warm them. On the back of her palm, it said, "I'll always be here" in dulled down ink. Brooke would later get it tattooed over his hand writing.

"Daaad, I'm home."

"Where'd you go?" Peter called from the kitchen.

Brooke tried to get up the stairs as fast as she could. "To the park."

"Why? You haven't even eaten anything. And your class starts in fifteen minutes!" Brooke wasn't one to pull a classic teenager on him. She hadn't done that since like freshman year.

"I'm exercising my right not to go to class."

Long silence.

"But I'm making pancakes!"

Brooke's door closed quietly. So quietly that Peter and May could hear the lock from downstairs clicking into place and her coat falling to the floor. Then she turned up a song Jace had shown her one day.

> *Like a gunshot from miles away*
> *She's moving in*
> *Like a rainstorm without the clouds*
> *She falls on him*
> *Like a phone call to worn the truth*
> *It never rings*
> *It's the truth before the lies*
> *It's the way she doesn't try*
> *It's the wink before the slight*
> *In Philadelphia*
> *In Philadelphia*

"Ooh. Love this song."

"Okay, Jace. Ridiculous."

"Yeees?" There was a wind chime set up by her window, and now that Brooke acknowledged his half alive half dead existence, he got to mess with it. He ran his bony fingers around it.

Brooke let out a long sigh. She sat on the bed, by the window, where she assumed he was. Her face fell into her hands. "You're ridiculous."

"I know. What's your point? God, I'm so sarcastic when I'm dead. I wish you could hear me, you'd be totally rolling your eyes right now." A nice little tune played along with Philadelphia until he noticed her.

"Wait, why are you upset? Why do I say all of these things out loud? Do you think there are other ghosts that can hear me and they think I'm talking to them?"

She let out another long, shaky sigh.

"Shit, right, sorry."

Jace didn't know what to do. He just wanted more time, occasionally, to reassure her of his presence. Or touch her hand, or kiss her lips or anything. Anything. He would do anything. He would play with her hair if he could. Instead, he tried to play with her hair. "Oh, shit, I hope this doesn't weird you out."

He took a deep breath. "I'm not good at flirting. Don't forget about that. I never learned how to braid. Shit. I'm gonna try it." His hands shook in his nervousness.

Her blonde hair fell a little bit past her shoulders,

and she usually wore it up. Right now, it was up in a pony tail. Jace slowly pulled the scrunchie down from her hair. He was trying to make it discreet, but apparently, he would learn it wasn't possible to take out a hair scrunchie without alerting the person about it.

And he would learn this the hard way.

Brooke's hand flew backwards and she attempted to back hand whatever crazy ass cat burglar decided to come into her house and braid her hair. It did just fly through Jace's face, but it scared the shit out of him

"Whoa, whoa. Nemo, it's just me." He continued to braid her hair in a ragged, confused fashion.

Brooke tried to relax. "You're being weird."

"I know, I know. But I wanna treat you nice and everything. It's the least I could do, considering you just broke up with your boyfriend for me. You just broke up with your boyfriend for a dead guy. And you call me ridiculous, you're crazy."

She relaxed. She didn't say anything, and was content doing so.

And they just sat there like that. She missed her architecture three hundred and five class and it was totally worth it. The last time she took a day off was... Never. And there was no one she would rather be spending her day off with than with her dead boyfriend.

Peter finished his pancakes and tried his best not to come up the stairs with the dad-liest questions, complete with the "I'm knocking to respect your privacy but I'm asserting my responsibility as a parent and coming in any way!" He saw a weird thing.

Not the weirdest thing he ever saw. He did meet a southern gay trucker outside of a hospital room one time, but he never actually told that story to anyone. It was something he liked to keep to himself. "You've got a ghost braiding your hair or something?"

It was a joke but it scared the shit out of Jace. "Did you tell him? You can't run around telling everyone I'm a ghost, it'll ruin my plans to mess with everyone. I was planning on going to Travis's house and screwing with some stuff but if he hears that it's me, it won't be any fun!" One thing did not change from life to death; how much Jace Aiko Anderson would not stop talking.

Brooke, in the hospital, liked to tell him he just liked listening to the sound of his own voice. "Just like your dad. Didn't your dad have that voice?"

"I don't know, I don't really remember."

Jace liked to space out and talk a lot and get entirely off topic.

"W-what?" Brooke jumped. "No. I... I braided it

and I decided to lay here. Yep. That's it."

"Alright, what's up, Nemo? I brought you pancakes, too. And the syrup. And a fork."

Brooke forced a laugh, taking the plate from her father. "Thanks, Dad, really. I'm starving anyway."

"Why'd you go to the park, hun? How did your date with what's his name go last night?"

She took a long, borderline annoyed breath. "He proposed to me..."

"He proposed to you?!"

"And I said no."

"... And you said no."

"And I said no." Brooke laughed.

Laughter after a denied proposal? God, there is definitely something wrong with her, Peter thought.

"I said no, because I'm still not over this boy who brought me flowers and tripped over his own feet. And he's dead, Dad." Brooke just stared at her pancake.

Peter and Jace could feel the breakdown coming from miles away. Both wanted to prevent it, but only Peter could do something. "Look, don't beat yourself up over it, okay? He was really great."

"He was really great, huh?"

"He was. I loved him. You guys laughed at him and not at me."

Brooke wiped the back of her hand across her nose and started to revert into a child like position, with a blanket around her shoulders and her knees pulled up to her chest. "But how could I-"

"No buts."

"But I-"

"Stop. There was no way you could've known he was telling the truth. Your mom still doesn't believe it, but she doesn't even believe in Bigfoot, so she doesn't count for anything."

Brooke shook her head, "no. I mean... I think he's still here. I think he gave up whatever he had to help me. Heaven or whatever." Saying it out loud just made her more sure that she was losing her mind and she should just settle down with a nice guy. "And I just turned my back on him."

Peter didn't know what to say. He set her pancakes on her nightstand with the fork and the syrup on the side. "Well... I'm gonna tell you the same thing that I told a gay trucker one time in the hospital."

"A gay trucker?"

"Mmhmm. A gay, southern trucker. He had really messed up, I'm not really sure what he did... But I'm pretty sure it wasn't that good. Anyway... What was it exactly?" He took a couple of deep breaths.

"I'm a master in screwing up, and therefore, I have to be a master in fixing things."

Brooke couldn't help but roll her eyes. She must've heard that hundreds, if not thousands of times in her life. Sometimes it was phrased differently, with an expletive in the middle, but it was always the same thing. "Dad, you told me that when I failed AP Chemistry. I don't think this is really the same thing."

"I don't care," her father said. "You know how to fix things. I know you can and I know you will. It's a shame you're not marrying what's-his-face but you know what's best for you. Stop doubting yourself."

And with that, Peter kissed her head and took the pancakes back downstairs and left his little girl to think for herself. That's what she was best at.

Epilogue

2028

"I can't believe you're really doing this. I know you're like, 29 and all, but I still picture you as being seventeen."

Over ten years of following Brooke around later, Jace still hadn't run out of things to say. Actually, he wasn't even close.

Brooke knew what he was saying and signed the papers anyway. She did know what she was doing. She was a successful independent architect and interior designer so she had plenty of money and always knew this is what she wanted.

May didn't approve of Brooke's decision and she made a point of showing it, by not showing up to the party at Brooke's house.

It was a surprise party; in the way that everyone would be surprised to learn why they were there.

Peter knew, of course, and was still limber enough to decorate with great enthusiasm. Decorating was the only thing keeping him from blurting out his daughter's secret to the gathered family members and coworkers. *She'll be home any minute.*

Shit.

Jace sat in the front seat of her car, buckled himself in, and listened to a Parachute song on the radio. It was his routine and he was a little too frustrated to babble. He didn't understand why Brooke was doing this. There were thousands of easier ways to go about it, but she picked one of the hardest.

Typical Brooke.

The minute Peter ran out of blue streamers, he heard Brooke's car pulling into the driveway. Everyone got into place for Brooke's big announcement, squishing together in the living room of the modest little house.

And Peter waited by the door.

Jace walked behind Brooke. "I mean, I don't know if I'm ready for this. I should be included as part of the decision."

She was just smiling as she parked, running her hand through her hair. "You'll be fine," she murmured to him. "I know you will."

And Peter waited.

And waited.

And waited.

The secret was killing him. He couldn't keep secrets to save his life. *Brooke better get in here soon or*

I'm gonna spill the beans and she'll be mad at me, but it'll be her fault.

Brooke's front door swung open before she could reach for it with her spare hand, and she assumed it was Jace until Peter poked out from behind the door; wide eyed, beaming, happier than ever, proud of his daughter but even more so of his decorating skills. "So… Where's the-"

Before Peter could get ahead of himself, Brooke addressed the party. From behind her back, she pulled a bassinet and set it on the table.

"I'd like everyone to meet my adopted son, Jace."

Jace's Playlist

Sinking like a Stone by For The Foxes
Philadelphia by Parachute
Savant Song by Douglas II
Grapefruit by Aaron West and the
Roaring Twenties
Remembering Sunday by All Time low
Always Summer by Yellowcard
Ghost by Damion Suomi
Newport by Soren Bryce